HERCULES
THE LEGENDARY JOURNEYS™

THE FIRST CASUALTY

A novel by David L. Seidman

**based on the Universal television series
created by Christian Williams**

**Executive produced by Sam Raimi
and Robert Tapert**

BOULEVARD BOOKS, NEW YORK

HERCULES: THE LEGENDARY JOURNEYS: THE FIRST CASUALTY

A novel by David L. Seidman, based on the Universal television series HERCULES: THE LEGENDARY JOURNEYS, created by Christian Williams.

HERCULES: THE LEGENDARY JOURNEYS ™ & © 1997 MCA Television Limited. All rights reserved. Executive produced by Sam Raimi and Robert Tapert.

A Boulevard Book / published by arrangement with MCA Publishing Rights, a Division of MCA, Inc.

PRINTING HISTORY
Boulevard edition / April 1997

The Putnam Berkley World Wide Web site address is
http://www.berkley.com/berkley

Make sure to check out *PB Plug*, the science fiction/fantasy newsletter, at
http://www.pbplug.com

ISBN: 1-57297-239-4

BOULEVARD
Boulevard Books are published by The Berkley Publishing Group,
200 Madison Avenue, New York, New York 10016.
BOULEVARD and its logo are trademarks
belonging to Berkley Publishing Corporation.

PRINTED IN THE UNITED STATES OF AMERICA

10 9 8 7 6 5 4 3 2 1

To my, brother, Mark,
and my sister, Stacey,
two of the most honest people I know.

Acknowledgments

Many thanks:

To William Messner-Loebs, writer, cartoonist and scholar, for advice on Greek mythology.

To Debra Mostow-Zakarin, the book's first editor, for hiring me.

To Cindy Chang, the book's second editor, for her aid in getting the job finished.

To Barry Neville, the book's third editor, for his professionalism and unfailing courtesy.

To Paul Levine, my lawyer, for his aid with the contract and general support.

To Louise Wilson, my high-school Latin teacher, for pounding information about ancient days into my head. *Mundus semper erit gratus iste capitis ornatis.*

The first casualty when war comes is truth.

HIRAM JOHNSON
(U.S. POLITICIAN, 1866–1945)

1

The demigoddess Dryope the Beautiful, Queen of the Forest Nymphs, sat on a throne of polished oak and pine, watching a ring of wood sprites frolic around her in a dance of praise and adoration. As the slim, lithe girls leaped and pranced and swooped, occasionally bursting out in tinkling laughs of golden joy, their queen had but a single thought: *If I don't find something exciting to do, I will rip these obnoxious little fairies from their skinny legs.*

The queen began to sigh but clamped her lips shut. Queens, she knew, had their role, and hers was to let her nymphs glorify her. Actually, she had found the dances and songs of worship very sweet the first time she had heard them, and the second, and even the nineteenth—but after the first few centuries, they grew dull. Wood nymphs were lovely creatures but short on imagination; they repeated themselves with tiresome frequency and at nearly endless length.

Dryope bit her lip, hoping that the pain would keep her awake. Nevertheless, her eyelids began to slide down, bringing blissful darkness. Slowly, her shoulders slumped and her head tilted forward.

"O, our Queen, do we, thy servants, displease thee?" wailed the lead dancer, Prissia. "Hurry, my sisters. We must redouble our efforts to inspire Her Glorious Majesty!"

Dryope jerked up and blinked herself awake. *No, no, no, NO!*, she thought, but she kept silent. She knew from ugly experience not to criticize the nymphs. The first time she had tried, her words threw the girls into a sulky, week-long pout; since the girls were forest spirits, their bad mood sent blights, molds, and a gray fungus throughout the forest. Dryope had had to let the nymphs dance about her for twice as long as usual before they felt better. Since then, she had never let the slightest displeasure pass her lips.

"From the beginning, my sisters!" Prissia cried. Her shrill trill scratched inside the queen's ear like a dirty fingernail. The sprites raised thin, wispy scarves and rose high on pointed toes. "And one, and two—"

"What manner of creatures are these?" called a rough, guttural voice from deep in the forest.

The dancers froze. "Thank Hera," Dryope muttered. *Time to go to work*, she thought.

She rose smoothly from her throne, forcing herself not to stretch her arms and legs, stiffened by sitting still for the past hour. She gazed levelly into the for-

2

est. "Show yourself and name your name," she demanded.

His boots crushing leaves and worms on the soft forest ground, a man strode from behind a tight stand of trees. As Prissia and the other nymphs squealed and fled behind the queen's throne, Dryope took the man's measure.

Smells pretty good for a mortal, she thought. Humans, especially ones who tramped through the forest, usually stank like goats. One could smell them coming.

Not this one, though. He was big, taller than a stallion, taller than Dryope herself. Black, curly hair covered his broad form, from his wide shoulders and burly chest to his bulging calves. On the man's thigh, a red scar like a cobra's head caught Dryope's eye. His only clothing was the skin of a lion across his body, tied at his right shoulder and left leg. His fingers, each thick as a boar's tusk, wrapped around a gleaming dagger; a blood-spattered sword hung from one hip.

She noticed him scanning her as she was assessing him. His dark eyes swept boldly down her snowy skin and slim figure. *The big animal's not even trying to hide his interest*, Dryope thought. It took considerable effort to keep a sly smile off her lips.

"General?" called a soft voice from the area where the man had first appeared.

A young man emerged from behind the stand of trees that had hid the first man. The new man was slim, his skin pink from a fresh sunburn. He wore the too-tight skin of a fawn. He tugged at the knot that

3

held it in place at his hip, trying to loosen the knot without undoing it entirely. "General, we're standing exposed here, and you did tell us that the Pastoralians could attack at any time."

"Shut up, Honorius," the general growled, continuing to stare at Dryope.

"Begging your pardon, sir," the young man said quietly, "but no." He stopped fiddling with the knot and stood straight as an iron rod. In firm tones, he went on, "The men are exhausted from the march you've put them through today. I want to dig trenches here. We'll escape the Pastoralians' notice and get a chance to bed down."

The general kept looking at Dryope, drinking in her blonde hair and blazing blue eyes. "No," he said. "March the men a mile from here. I want privacy when I—confer with the the lovely lady before us." He flashed a gleaming grin at Dryope, who lowered her long lashes and smiled demurely at him. "Make it five miles," he said.

The younger man took a deep breath and stepped in front of the general. Looking him directly in the eyes, he continued, "General Ferocius, sir, the men are tired. A march would—"

The general grabbed Honorius by the chest and shoved him against a tree. The rough bark ripped into the younger man's tender, sunburned flesh. He quietly winced.

Ferocius tightened his clutch on Honorius' chest and dug his nails into the younger man's rosy skin. The general leaned close and growled, "Shut up, you little—"

4

"Leave him alone," a deep voice called.

Ferocius whirled, dropping Honorius. He saw a tall, bronzed man striding through the forest. The muscles of the stranger's arms bulged as big as pine cones; his chest was as broad as a door; his legs were as thick as oak trunks.

But more fearsome was his expression. Clenched tight with anger, his face was as grim as a storm cloud; his eyes flashed as if full of lightning.

"Hercules," Ferocius whispered.

Dryope stared at the big man stepping toward them. While Ferocius was a wild bear, all brutality and force, the man before them moved with the smooth power of a lion leading a pride across the veldt, sure in his ability to handle any challenge. Under his off-white shirt, she suspected, lurked a passionate heart.

Mmmm, she thought. *Yummy*.

She glanced at Ferocius, who was watching as the stranger helped Honorius to his feet, pulled a poultice from the bag slung around his neck, and applied it to Honorius' bleeding back. Suddenly uninterested in the general, she turned her gaze to the newcomer.

"Oh, *Hercules*," she called, every syllable a musical note. She crooked a finger at the man. "Come here. I'd like to . . . chat with you." She sat down gracefully and crossed her strong, slim legs. Behind her, the wood nymphs giggled.

"Don't do it, Hercules," Ferocius said suddenly, shaking his head as if to clear it. "She'll ensnare you with her beauty. She nearly got me before you came along.

"Come back with us, Hercules," he urged.

"We've got a war brewing, and I could use your help. My city-state would be grateful." In low tones, he added, "If it's women you like, we have women who make Blondie up there look like last month's cow pies, if you know what I mean."

"I'll help if I can," said the man with the gleaming muscles. "Another time, Your Majesty."

Ferocius led his quest into the misty woods. Honorius followed, troubled but obedient.

Crouching behind the wooden throne, Prissia looked up. She saw her beloved queen grip the thick arms of her throne. The queen rose, tearing the arms off with a sharp snap. She squeezed, and the arms burst into splinters. She shrieked terrible curses.

Prissia looked at the scowling face of her queen and performed the bravest act of her life: she spoke up. "Your Majesty? I know you're upset, and, well, we'd like to make you feel better . . . so . . ." She took a deep breath. "Hit it, girls!"

As a dozen dryads danced about her, singing a hymn about the beauty of Dryope's nose, the queen sank back onto her throne and buried her head in her hands. She looked up, straightened her gown, and concentrated on a single thought: *You're going to pay for this, Hercules*.

2

One month later, Hercules sat on a beach of the Greek island of Peloponnesus, watching a boat float off into the Gulf of Corinth and listening to his friend Salmoneus the peddler hurl loud, futile curses at its skipper. The demigod remembered his father.

Zeus, king of the gods, had a temper as powerful as the lightning bolts that he hurled from Olympus. When he raged, the earth shook.

Zeus's wife, Hera, could hold a grudge for decades. Ever since Hercules was born, she had hated the sight of him because Zeus fathered him with another woman; frequently, she tried to kill him.

Ares, the god of war and Hercules' half brother, would spark conflicts that took the lives of thousands of humans and left millions homeless simply because he couldn't get fresh grapes for breakfast and wanted to take his frustration out on somebody. *Heck, I've even got some special talents of my own*, Hercules thought. *But no one can swear like Salmoneus.*

"—and the boat you rode in on!" Salmoneus concluded. He grabbed fistfuls of beach sand and hurled them at the small boat.

The wind blew the sand back in his face. Salmoneus coughed and sputtered; he rubbed his eyes to get the sand out (succeeding only in rubbing the sand in) and looked for a rock big enough to throw at the boat. "Dump *us*, will he?" he raged. "Some boatman. I swear, just because there's a little war going to start, he gets all cowardly." He grabbed the hem of his toga and shook some of the sand out.

"Relax, Salmoneus," Hercules said. "He did tell us about this place."

Hercules looked around. For an island on the brink of battle, it seemed quiet. No one else was on the beach; the sands led up to a deep forest where the only sounds were the chirps of a few birds.

The sun was setting over the water. They had best find shelter soon. He started walking toward the forest, with Salmoneus following behind.

"It's not the boatman's fault you couldn't nag him into showing us around," Hercules went on. "After all, it *is* a war zone."

Salmoneus stepped toward the trees, peering forward, alert for trouble. "I never knew you were so brave, Salmoneus," Hercules observed.

"Oh, I don't actually intend to get *hurt* in the war," Salmoneus replied.

"Of course," Hercules agreed with a slight smile.

He looked around for signs of trouble. He saw none. *If this is a war zone, why is it so calm?* he thought. *I don't like it. Was the boatman lying to us?*

Salmoneus was still talking, ignoring the slightly mocking tone in his friend's voice. "I just plan to stick around, sop up some local color, pick up a few wild stories. Then I'm back to Athens before the fighting begins. I write a few scrolls about the island, and bingo! I'm a freshly minted expert on war-torn Peloponnesus. All I have to do is get my tales on the *New Athens Times* best-seller list, and it's the big time for me: lecture tours, high speaking fees, and this new thing that's happening in the amphitheaters: it's called a 'talk show.'"

His tone turned dreamy. "One appearance on Jayos Lenodiis' show, and I'll be famous all over the Greek Isles. And with fame," Salmoneus added in a sharper tone, "come drachmas, shekels, dinars—I don't care what you call it as long as I can spend it."

Whatever you say, Salmoneus, Hercules thought. He listened for danger.

He heard the sounds of movement in the forest.

He caught a glimpse of a short figure moving through the woods. A clump of trees blocked him from seeing the person clearly; the growing dimness of dusk made a clear view even harder.

Who was it?

Pan, maybe, Hercules thought. *He's a short god, a forest god, and Peloponnesus is one of his homes. Better approach carefully; he's a tricky one.* Hercules reviewed the god's abilities. *God of fertility; that could be dangerous. One blast on those pipes he plays, and I'd be hip deep in sheep or poison ivy, growing faster than I could handle.*

"Herc?" Salmoneus interrupted his thoughts.

"Sh!" Hercules hissed. He pointed at the figure at the forest and followed it into the trees.

"This is great!" Salmoneus whispered. "Action already. Jayos Lenodiis, here I come."

"Quiet, Salmoneus," Hercules murmured. "This could be dangerous."

"Aw, you can handle it, Herc," Salmoneus soothed. "Don't you get it? My tales need excitement, adventure, danger!"

A dozen soldiers burst out of the woods from all sides. Screaming and charging, they thrust bloody lances at the two men.

Hercules ducked, but Salmoneus remained standing, frozen like a deer caught in the torchlights of an oncoming chariot. Hercules grabbed the peddler by the toga front and yanked him, tumbling, to the dewy ground. *Fooled*, Hercules thought. *Decoyed. Suckered!*

He looked up, expecting that the soldiers, without a standing body to hit, had neatly skewered each other, as men who attack in a circle often do. But the soldiers were smarter than usual. They had arranged themselves so that their long lances stabbed between them, piercing only the empty air.

The soldiers pulled back for another charge. *There's something weird about them*, Hercules thought. He tried to see their expressions, but the fading light and the face-guards of their battle helmets—crisscrossing gates of bone—hid them thoroughly. Hercules did notice the daggers strapped to their sides

10

and the dried blood staining their lances' sharp tips.

He also noticed that the soldiers looked short, but that didn't matter. The pygmies of central Africa were short but fierce and deadly.

Still holding Salmoneus by the toga, Hercules leaped skyward. He shot up, the leafy treetops brushing his face, and grabbed a thick, long branch. It cracked under his weight but held. "Excitement, adventure, danger?" he muttered to Salmoneus as they hung in midair, swaying.

"Well, yeah—for other people," the peddler sniveled.

"Fire!" a high-pitched voice shouted, and Hercules saw the soldiers fling their lances at his face. The weapons whistled through the air.

Hercules let the limb go. He and Salmoneus plummeted as the lances struck only the air and the tree.

They hit the ground hard. Hercules grabbed Salmoneus' wrists and flung the peddler, screaming, back up into the branches. *Grab one and stay safe, Salmoneus,* Hercules thought.

He turned to face the soldiers, who were fanning out to surround him. They instantly formed a double circle, one ring of six soldiers inside the other. They pulled out their daggers, and charged.

Hercules leaped like a pouncing jaguar and landed on the nearest soldier. He ripped off the soldier's helmet.

The freckled face of a blue-eyed boy, tall for his age but no older than fourteen, stared up at him, terrified and trembling.

"Halt!" a man's voice shouted.

The soldiers froze. Hercules looked around through the last flecks of dusky twilight and located the source of the voice: a sunburned man wearing the plumed helmet of a platoon commander, walking toward them from deep in the woods.

The man was slim and his face was unlined, but Hercules noted the dark circles of exhaustion under his eyes, the hard set of his mouth, and the lumpy scab over a gash on his otherwise smooth, sunburned right cheek. The man's iron breastplate was nicked and pitted in several places where knives, rocks, and other weapons had tried to pierce it. His right hand gripped a lance; his left hand held a dagger. The smallest finger of that hand was a scarred, uneven stump, and a bloody bandage of calfskin was wound tight around his forearm. Hercules noticed that the man limped slightly as he approached. Though shorter than Hercules, he was easily half a head taller than the tallest of the other soldiers.

Hercules stood up, letting the boy under him scramble to his feet. He turned to the commander. "What's going on here?"

"Don't speak unless I want you to," the man said. His voice was slow and rough; it dropped off to a soft slur at the end of his sentences, as if he hadn't the vigor to finish at full volume and clarity. The last time Hercules had heard such a voice was his own after he had cleaned out the Augean stables. After that nearly endless drudgery, he had wanted to rest for a month.

The commander turned to the boy Hercules had pinned. "Peuris," he said quietly, "what did your mother and I tell you about going out at night?''

"Aw, Dad," the boy said, "it wasn't night yet. And look, we almost got Hercules!"

How does he know who I am? Hercules wondered.

"Looks to me like you almost got him to kill you," the commander told the boy. He bent over and picked up a lance. "It also looks as if you and your friends stole this equipment from the armory."

"But no one was using it!" the boy wailed. "I mean, we're cadets, aren't we? That means we're soldiers in training! How are we ever going to get experience if we don't go out and—"

"Shush! Cadets, line up and stand at attention." As the boys formed two rows of six, the stranger turned to Hercules. "Now, as for you, why'd you come back here?"

"Come back?" Hercules asked. "I just got here. I've never been here before in my life."

The commander looked puzzled, as if Hercules had denied that he had two hands. "Why are you lying to me?" he asked, talking to himself as much as Hercules. "Maybe you don't remember me, but I was there when you met General Ferocius and the queen of the dryads."

"General who?" Hercules asked, equally puzzled.

One of the smallest boys broke out of the columns of cadets and approached the commander. "Captain Honorius," he squeaked, "begging your pardon, sir, but the general did order any and all soldiers to kill him on sight. I hate to tell you, sir, but you're in violation of orders number 77 Beta, 79 Alpha, 82 Epsi—"

"Thank you, Cadet Sycophantius," Honorius interrupted wearily. "I do know my orders. Now, get back in ranks, please." He turned toward Hercules. "You heard the cadet. Now, either stop lying or I'll kill you." With both hands, he aimed at Hercules the lance that he'd picked up from the forest floor. "I'm in no mood for idiocy."

With a whirl of leaves and a hard smash, Salmoneus crashed onto the ground between them. Rubbing his bruised bottom, the peddler looked up with a smile that he hoped was pitiable, charming, and lovable. "Lost my grip on the tree," he explained.

Captain Honorius did not find Salmoneus lovable. "Idiocy," he muttered. He looked at Hercules, who was helping Salmoneus to his feet. "Is this moron yours?"

"Hey!" Salmoneus shouted, shaking off Hercules' help. He stuck his face close to Honorius', ready to defend his injured honor. "Who are you calling—"

Eight cadets scrambled toward Salmoneus. Hercules clamped a hand over his friend's mouth and pulled him back. Honorius raised a palm like a police officer signaling a stop, and the boys halted.

"He's my friend. He's harmless," Hercules told the captain. "But if you want to kill me, then why should I expect you to believe what I say?"

The captain sighed. "I didn't say that I wanted to kill you. The cadet said that my general had ordered us to kill you." He looked Hercules over from toes to forehead and settled on his eyes. "But if you've really spent the last two weeks among the enemy, then you've got valuable information. I may get run through, but this is one time to risk disobeying my leader. Cadet Peuris!''

The captain's son came trotting forward and saluted smartly. ''Yes, sir?''

''We're going back to town. Get four men around each prisoner, two men up front to scout the way, and two to bring up the rear.'' He turned away.

''Yes, sir,'' Peuris said, and saluted again. He prodded Hercules with the point of his sword. ''Stand still, you,'' he grunted. ''Cadet Sycophantius!'' he called. ''Eight men, including yourself, on the double. And bring rope!'' He glared at Hercules and Salmoneus. ''The rough twine we use to drag oxen!'' he added, grinning. ''You'll just adore the twine, mister,'' he told Hercules. ''Raw hemp, triple strength. I've seen it scrape a bull's hide right off. Probably slice through your baby wrists like a hot knife through soft cheese.''

''Knock it off, son,'' the captain said from eight feet away. His tone was mild, but it shot through the boy like a sudden chill. ''This is Hercules, remember. You've heard of his powers. Your twine can't bother him, so don't be silly.''

''Yes, sir,'' Peuris said softly, chastened. His voice cracked. Boys surrounded Hercules and Salmoneus at north, south, east and west. The front and rear guards pulled dry branches off the ground and rubbed them together until they struck flame. Using the branches as torches, the group marched into the night.

Hercules glanced over at Salmoneus, who was trying to find a way to take notes on their exploits. He reached into his shoulder bag for a quill and a small scroll, but Sycophantius and Peuris poked him with their swords.

"They probably think you're reaching for a weapon," Hercules said.

"It doesn't matter," Salmoneus replied. "I can always go from memory when I get back. 'I and my sidekick Hercules fought off the hardened barbarian soldiers, but Hercules—a good-hearted fellow, but not as clever as I—got us taken prisoners.' You don't mind my embellishing things a bit, do you, pal?"

"Quiet," Honorius grunted. Salmoneus shut up.

But something that Salmoneus said tickled Hercules' curiosity. "Captain, I've got a question," he called into the night. "You're under orders to kill me. What for? What do your people think I did?"

Honorius' voice cut through the darkness: "Treason."

3

The word startled Hercules. Salmoneus stared at him in shock. "You did *what*?" the peddler asked.

"I didn't do anything. Captain, this doesn't make sense," Hercules insisted. "There's only one way I could commit treason, and that's if I was a citizen of your country who went over to your enemy's side. I'm not a citizen. I told you, I've never been here in my life."

For a moment, the captain was silent. "My city-state," he began, "is named Mercantilius. Our people are merchants and traders. Always have been."

Several weeks back, he continued, trade dropped off. Someone was spreading lies: that Mercantilians were refusing to pay for shipments, that they willfully damaged trade goods, that they lied about shipping quantities and delivery dates.

The largest town on the island, Mercantilius dropped from being one of the richest to one of the poorest. Fewer and fewer people would trade with the Mercantilians. Businesses that had flourished for generations closed down. Mercantilian families that had always prospered began going hungry. Landlords forced out tenants who could no longer pay their rent; soon after, the landlords had to sell their buildings, because no one could afford to rent there. And the landlords went broke, since they could find no one with enough money to buy their buildings.

Ebon Ferocius, chief of the city-state's small police force, tracked down the source of the rumors. They came from Pastoralis, Peloponnesus' second largest city-state, a town of shepherds and ranchers.

"It didn't make sense," Honorius said. "We'd been trading with Pastoralis for years. Oh, there were disputes—my father was once mayor of our city, and he had had a terrible fight with Slaughterius, the Pastoralian mayor, over differences between the towns' currencies. But that was nothing like this. They'd never spread lies about us before."

But now they had. Mercantilians, as well as people from other towns, had heard them do it.

The Pastoralians denied the charge. What's more, to the shock of the Mercantilians, the Pastoralians accused *them* of spreading lies that were ruining the Pastoralians' trade.

"They said terrible things. They said we told other towns that Pastoralian sheep were diseased and would poison anyone who ate them or wore their wool; that

18

Pastoralian steers were infested with insects too tiny to see; that the milk from Pastoralian cows and goats would cause children who drank it to cease growing. And they had proof! Witnesses, letters, sworn testimony—all lies and forgeries, of course, but we couldn't prove that.

"I used to see that sort of thing all the time when my father judged lawsuits as town leader," the captain went on. "Let's say Citizen A accuses Citizen B of a crime. The fastest way the accused man can go from being on the defensive to being on the side of righteousness is to accuse his accuser. If you say that your accuser is guilty of some terrible offense, suddenly everyone stops thinking about you. They start to wonder if your accuser is guilty and can't be trusted."

Hercules nodded. The gods, he remembered, did the same thing when he was a boy. Hades, the god of the dead, had accused Hermes, god of thieves, of stealing the ferryboat that carried the dead to Hades' underworld. Hermes retaliated by saying that Hades had hired the war god Ares to start a war that would increase Hades' supply of the dead. A number of gods disliked Hades to begin with—Artemis publicly called him "a cold-faced, stinky-breathed old creep"—and tossed in their own accusations, forgetting the question of whether or not Hermes was guilty of stealing Hades' ferry. The situation, with its petty jealousies and rampant lies, remained one of the ugliest memories of Hercules' youth.

In any event, the Mercantilians didn't like the Pastoralians calling them slanderers. Arguments got hot, demands for apologies were made and refused.

The Pastoralians looked hungry, angry, and desperate enough to do anything. The Mercantilians turned their police force into an army and named Ferocius its general. He sent patrols to circle the city and its surrounding forests, looking for trouble.

"Begging the captain's pardon," said a young cadet wearing a backpack, "but can I say something? My dad was on one of those patrols—a night patrol, it was—when suddenly, these things came slingshotting at us out of the forest. My dad gave it to me."

He pulled a thick club out of his backpack and handed it to Hercules. The club was heavy and sharpened to a point, with a sword blade stuck into the top.

The cadet went on, "They—the Pasters—use these things a lot. Every soldier fixes it up special. I saw one shaped like a giant bear's claw, and another that had a big net attached to it—"

"And another with an ax blade stuck in the side," the squeaky-voiced Sycophantius interrupted. "And there was another with a real thin shell and a lot of glue inside, so when it hit something, the shell cracked and whatever it hit got all gooped up, and there was one that—"

"An unprovoked attack," Captain Honorius summarized. "The clubs came flying over our city walls. Some of them hit our school. If they'd attacked during the day, they might have killed children.

"At dawn, a whole platoon of Pasters came boiling over a high ridge that separates our city from theirs. They were howling for revenge."

"Revenge?" Salmoneus asked. "For a few rumors?"

"No," Honorius said. "They claimed that we *stole* their clubs and then attacked their people. They found our spears near their dead bodies.

"We got that bit of news from a couple of Paster prisoners we caught. Now, our men have left spears in the forest after hunting trips and practice battles, so someone may have used them to kill those Pastoralians—but we didn't do it.

"In any event, we drove the Pasters off—but we have spies who tell us they'll be back, and with more than one hastily assembled platoon. It's total war now."

"Okay," said Salmoneus, "but what's this got to do with Hercules? He didn't start the war."

"He did worse than that!" Peuris cried, bolting forward. "He was terrible!"

"Quiet, son," the captain said softly. "Get back in ranks. I was there. I'll tell it."

Hercules, Honorius said, had entered the scene when General Ferocius was leading a platoon to find and destroy a patrol of Pastoralians that (rumor had it) were lurking in the forests near Mercantilius. The patrol had stumbled across the Queen of the Dryads and her court of nymphs when Hercules had entered. Ferocius persuaded Hercules to come back to town with them and join the Mercantilian side of the war.

"That's when the trouble started," Honorius said. "We offered you the town's hospitality, and you took it. Food, ale, wenches, our softest beds and most attentive servants—surely you remember.

21

"We didn't mind at first; we knew you could help us. For years, travelers had told us tales of your great deeds, your mighty powers, your superhuman abilities. All you had to do was face off against the Pastoralians, and they were as good as dead.

"So you ate and drank and rested; we figured you were gathering your strength for the ordeal to come. Soldiers like me drilled day and night for the attack that we expected you to lead. We were on our worst rations—the best being reserved for you, of course—but we didn't mind, not with victory on its way. Everyone in town was ready to cheer you on." He paused. "Especially the children."

"And then you ran away!" Peuris shouted. He collected himself. "It wasn't fair," he mumbled.

For a moment, the only sound was the soft crackling of the torches and the tramping of boots on the cool ground. The captain's reminder of Hercules' treachery had sobered everyone.

Everyone but Salmoneus. "Are you nuts?" he cried. "Hercules wouldn't do anything like that. Tell 'em, Herc."

"Let him finish, Salmoneus," Hercules said. There was something wrong with Honorius' story, but Hercules didn't want to start arguing until he had all the facts.

"There's not much more to say," the captain went on. "It seemed that the Pastoralian 'prisoners' we took were actually spies the Pastoralians planted. They wrote you a message that the Pasters could offer you more and better luxuries than we did. You must

22

have accepted. On the third dawn after you arrived in our city, you were gone."

"You stabbed my big brother," Sycophantius said. Everyone else fell silent.

"He was guarding the house we gave you," Sycophantius went on. "You shoved one of those clubs that the Pasters use right into his heart."

"So General Ferocius ordered you to kill me," Hercules concluded thoughtfully. "From your viewpoint, it makes sense."

Salmoneus gaped. "Are you actually agreeing with these yokels?" he shouted. A sword's point jabbed the peddler's ribs. "No offense," Salmoneus said. "Where I come from, 'yokel' is, um, a term of praise used to describe people who—provincial and simple though they might be—are truly fine folk, the salt and the pepper and indeed the very nutmeg of the earth, nature's own aristocrats, the finest—." Another poke in the ribs, a sharper one; Salmoneus quieted down.

It does make sense, Hercules thought. *But how can there be another one of me running around?* Pretenders to Hercules' fame were common. Since accurate portraits were rare, any hulk with a big mouth could claim to be the Greek Isles' greatest hero. The only people who weren't fooled were those who had seen the real man close up, and they were a tiny minority.

But these soldiers had seen both Hercules and the person claiming to be him, and they thought that the two men were the same one. *I can't have a twin out there*, Hercules thought. *I'd have heard.*

Or would I?

"We're here," Honorius said. Up ahead was a

long, rough wall of logs, glued together with dried clay. Of uneven height and thickness, the logs leaned against each other.

Hercules guessed that the Mercantilians had put up the wall in haste as the war drew nearer. Clearly, they'd never needed any such defense before and were new at building such things.

A section of the wall angled open. Hercules could see men pushing it from the inside. From the town a cadet marched toward Captain Honorius; the boy stopped and saluted. As Honorius returned the salute, Hercules realized that the boy must have been one of Peuris' advance scouts. He had run ahead to the city and informed the citizens that the captain was coming back with a special prisoner.

A tall, burly man marched out through the door, attended by an honor guard of a dozen full-grown soldiers. Like Honorius, he wore a breastplate and plumed helmet; but his breastplate was of gleaming silver, not of the dull iron that Honorius wore. The feathers on his helmet were shining black, like a raven's wing, and taller than the sagging plumes on the captain's head. The sword hanging at his side was long and looked heavy.

The man's dark gaze locked onto Hercules. He strode past Honorius, ignoring the captain's salute and pushing him aside. As Honorius stumbled into a tree, the big man stood in front of Hercules and looked him up and down.

"I run this city," the man said. "My name is Ferocius."

"I'm Hercules," Hercules answered, extending a

friendly hand. Ferocius did not shake it. "I thought this city was run by a mayor," Hercules went on. "You look like a general."

Ferocius snorted. "I am a general. As you know. When you left to aid the enemy, I declared this town under a state of military emergency and placed it under military law. As the highest-ranking military officer, that means my law. And under my law, you should be dead."

Next to Hercules, Salmoneus piped up, "Look, whoever you had here earlier who betrayed you, it wasn't him. There are a lot of people out there who claim that they're Hercules. But I know this big lug. He really is Hercules, and I'll prove it."

"Thanks, Salmoneus," Hercules said. *Good ol' Salmoneus. Looking out for himself, to be sure, but always helpful in a pinch.*

"No sweat," Salmoneus replied with a casual wave. "Show 'em."

Hercules stared. "What?"

"You heard me. Show 'em. Do a feat of strength. Uproot the forest or something."

Hercules leaned in close. "Salmoneus," he growled through gritted teeth, "I can't uproot a whole forest."

"Well, do something," Salmoneus growled back. "If they behead you, then they'll wonder what I'm doing with you, and they'll behead me."

"Fine," Hercules grumbled. He looked around. Through the city's doorway, a large object caught his attention.

He started toward the doorway. A group of Ferocius' soldiers trotted ahead of him, pivoted smartly, blocked his path, and pointed spears in his face.

Hercules looked over his shoulder at Ferocius. "Do you mind?"

"Back off, boys—for now," the general grunted. They retreated, watching Hercules warily from a few feet away.

I'd better make this good, Hercules thought. Entering the city, he approached a massive boulder in the town square, taller than himself and wide as an elephant. It seemed an odd object to put in a spot where everyone would have to detour around it, but Hercules reasoned that it was simply too big for them to clear away.

He squatted down, stretched out his arms, and grabbed the rock from the bottom. He could hear murmurs from the crowd—cynical mumbles from the soldiers insulting his sanity, awed gasps from some of the cadets, and "Six drachmas says he bursts a blood vessel."

He gripped the boulder hard, his fingers piercing the stony surface. Slowly, they dug in deeper, cracking and crunching the boulder, making handholds where there had been only bumps and ridges.

The rock felt too soft and strangely lightweight, but with everyone watching, Hercules couldn't back off now. If he let go of the rock and made excuses about something wrong with it, he would only erode his reputation further. They would think that he was too weak to lift the rock. They would conclude that he wasn't really Hercules. They would call him a liar. And they would kill him.

Hercules sprang upward, swinging the boulder toward the star-filled sky, and let it go. For a moment, both of them were in midair, Hercules' body outstretched and still rising from his leap, the rock shooting like a snowball flung by a boy trying to nail a passing bird.

At the height of his leap, Hercules saw the rock fly past the moon. He came down in a crouch, knees bent to absorb the shock of hitting the ground, and bounced into a sprint.

It shouldn't have gone that high, he thought. *I didn't throw it that hard.*

Still running, he watched the boulder begin to fall. He hoped it wouldn't hurt anyone, but found that the Mercantilians were handling that problem for him. They were scattering in all directions, helmets flying off their heads as the boulder whistled downward.

Hercules shifted left, placing himself directly under the plummeting rock. He looked up; he saw it rocketing at him like a vulture swooping down to devour a mouse. Its shadow covered him. He swallowed and found his throat dry; he licked his lips and found them dry, too.

Hercules stretched out his arms, ready to catch the boulder. He flexed his knees, ready to bend and absorb the impact.

Easy, he thought. *Take it easy, be careful, bend with the blow. . . .*

The rock hit him and shattered. It crumbled into slivers and chunks of dry wood.

Hercules coughed smoky clouds of dust out of his throat and brushed his hands on his shirt, clapping off layers of dirt and paint. He took a deep breath and regretted it; the air was still full of dust.

What happened here? he asked himself. *Better play it cool.* Regaining his composure, he stepped over to Ferocius as the crowd gaped at him. He asked the general, "Now do you believe I'm Hercules?"

Ferocius was brushing dirt off of his breastplate. "No," he said. "First, anyone could have thrown that boulder; it was a fake, made of wood and painted rags, and completely hollow. Second, you just destroyed our secret weapon. Honorius!"

The younger man approached Ferocius from behind. "Yes, general?"

"Tell our visitor what that boulder was."

Honorius chewed a knuckle thoughtfully. "Sir, it's a military secret—"

"Not anymore," Ferocious snapped. "Tell him."

Honorius stood at full attention and looked at Hercules. "We had heard a tale of the Greeks giving a giant wooden horse to the Trojans. The Trojans took the horse, not realizing that it was full of Greek soldiers. The Greeks attacked and sacked Troy."

"I know," Hercules said. "Some friends of mine died there. What does this have to do with that rock?"

"It was the first in a new series of secret weapons," Honorius answered. "We built it to hold a soldier, plus food and drink and weapons. We would place dozens of boulders in various places near the enemy camp. During a battle, we could use the soldiers as reinforcements, ambushers, spies—"

"That's enough," Ferocious snarled. "That rock was an experiment, the first of the series. We sneaked

28

it into the town square to see if it could fool our townspeople—and it did. And a good thing, too; it took weeks to build a fake that looked convincing. And you destroyed it."

Behind Hercules, leaves crunched under the paws of forest wolves running in the night. Crickets chirped, and a lost dog wailed at the moon. And someone laughed—a high, fast cackle, like dry wood snapping and popping in a fireplace. The laughter stopped abruptly, as if the laugher realized that someone would hear him.

Hercules looked up. *Uh-oh. I know that laugh.*

But Ferocius was still talking. He fixed Hercules with a steely stare. "Give me one good reason why I shouldn't kill you."

"I'll give you a very good reason," Hercules said. "You're in danger, and you'll need my help.

"A god is following us."

4

"And he's planning something dangerous," Hercules finished. "Someone out there just now laughed at the idea of my screwing up your plans. The gods laugh at the idea of humans having *any* plans worth considering. They look at us the way little boys look at worms, as something that's fun to step on and crush."

A battle-hardened soldier, General Ferocius was neither easily frightened nor easily fooled. Hercules could see the skepticism in his expression. "I'm not lying," Hercules insisted. "I'm telling the truth."

"*Sure*, you are," Ferocius said. He folded his hands over his belly and smiled, shaking his head like a father catching his son in a harmless, completely obvious fib. "Tell me, truthful man—which god did you hear?" The men of his honor guard chuckled.

Hercules did not smile. "It sounded like Hermes,

but it could have been Ares; they're half brothers, and their voices sometimes sound alike. Or it could have been one of Hermes' sons, like Pan. Or maybe—"

"Shut up," Ferocius said. He did not move.

His honor guard kept still, as did the cadets and Honorius. Hercules and a nervous Salmoneus followed their example.

Silent minutes passed.

At last Ferocius spoke. "Well, we've stood out here in the open, waiting for Hermes or Ares or whoever to attack, as you've predicted. Well, now . . . I don't see any divine beings firing down lightning bolts or a rain of blood. If they're out there, why haven't they turned us into tree toads or something?"

"Maybe they're trying to make me look stupid," Hercules replied. Even as he said it, he realized that the comment made him seem lame and weak or even deceitful. "I don't have an answer," he said. It made him seem even worse.

Out in the darkness, someone sniffled.

"Who's that?" Hercules said. He whirled and looked around. "Who's crying?"

"Nobody," a young voice said. "Leave me alone!"

General Ferocius' honor guard rushed forward and poked their swords at Hercules' gut. He slapped the swords away. "For Zeus' sake, you can kill me later if you want. Some kid's upset. I don't mind if *you* don't like me, but kids matter." He called into the darkness, "Come out, wherever you are. I won't hurt you."

"Shut up, you fraud!" shouted a voice full of pain. Footsteps pounded into the forest.

Hercules sprinted like a deer, following the steps. The boy was moving fast—no doubt one of the longer-legged lads—and he knew this forest. But Hercules could see moonlight reflecting off an armored back, flashing as it moved.

Hercules leaped, tackled the boy, tucked himself and his catch into a somersault and bounded up to a full upright stance. He grabbed the boy by the shoulders and looked into his eyes. It was Peuris, his face streaked with a muddy trail of tears.

"Don't talk to me, you fake!" the boy shouted. He tried to wriggle free, but Hercules held firm.

"I'm not a fake, Peuris," he said calmly. "And frankly, I'm upset that you think I am."

"But you are, you liar!" Peuris screeched. He wiped his face with the back of his wrist. "Get your sick hands off me!"

Hercules let him go. Honorius had been following them, and the boy ran to his side. "Stop it, Peuris," Honorius said. "You're acting like a baby, not a cadet."

"I don't care! I only joined the army to fight alongside *him!*" the boy shouted. He choked back sobs and swallowed hard.

"What in Hades is going on?" Ferocius roared. He was marching toward the trio.

"This is my fault, sir," Honorius said. "Among some tribes, they tell their children of a man in a red suit who brings presents to good children every winter. Other tribes talk about a big rabbit who gives out

33

chocolate eggs or a beautiful sprite who takes their teeth and gives them silver coins.

"Well, my wife and I told our son tales of Hercules. You know the travelers' tales—of a great hero who helps the weak with his mighty powers. My boy, he—I don't mean to embarrass you, son, but it's the truth. He believed. He practically worshiped Hercules.

"Well, when *he* came along"—Honorius cocked a thumb at Hercules—"my son was . . . well, it was a dream come true for him. And now—"

"And now that he's seen what a lying fraud Hercules is, not once but over and over, it's too much for him," Ferocius concluded. "Well, I don't blame him."

He walked over to Peuris and wrapped an arm around him, pulling the lad to his side. He turned to Hercules. "Look at this boy. How can you do that to him? They say I'm a hard man, and I am, but I wouldn't destroy a boy's trust like this."

Gently, he patted the lad's shoulder. "It's all right, son. This man—this fraud—was impersonating a hero I believed in, too. But I'm afraid it's true.

"There is no Hercules."

"I'm with you," the boy said firmly. "I don't believe in Hercules." He looked up at Hercules, his face full of contempt. "I don't believe in anything."

"No!" Hercules shouted. Hurriedly dropping to his knees, he looked up at Peuris' tear-streaked face. "You've got to believe in something. And if it's me— well, then I'll prove myself. Name a feat, and I'll do it. That's a promise."

The boy looked skeptical. "Well . . . okay. Fly to the moon and bring me back a crater."

Salmoneus spoke up. "He's got you there, Herc."

"Shut up, Salmoneus. Peuris, believe me, no one can do that except a god."

"But I heard you could!" the boy protested. "Everyone says you can. Travelers come through town and—"

"And things get exaggerated in the telling. Try another one," Hercules said. He realized that all of the soldiers and cadets were surrounding them, as well as a growing number of curious townspeople. All eyes were focused on him.

"Okay," the boy said. "Can you read minds?"

"Well, no."

"Walk through walls?"

"Well . . ."

"Turn invisible?"

A townsperson spoke up: "Breathe fire?"

A cadet with a surprisingly deep voice suggested, "Summon spirits?"

The squeaky-voiced Sycophantius added, "Speak the language of animals?"

More voices joined them. "Can you command the winds?"

"See through mountains?"

"Turn water into wine?"

"Raise the dead?"

For the first time in years, Hercules wished that he was fighting the Minotaur or battling Cerberus. Even cleaning out the Augean stables would have been preferable to the barrage from the Mercantilians.

"No," he admitted. "I can't do any of those things."

"Then forget it," Ferocius said. "We've all heard of Hercules. We know what he can do. If he had been here, he would have been our friend. And you, sir, are no Hercules."

Several members of the honor guard pulled out their daggers. Additional soldiers joined them: the town's night watchmen, as well as others who had gathered to watch the night's events. A mean-looking soldier wearing a chain-mail glove grinned, revealing a mouth with more gaps than teeth. He stared at Hercules' ribs and licked his lips.

"Besides," said the general, "whatever your name is, you're still the one who betrayed this city and went over to the side of our enemies." He turned to his soldiers.

A light dawned behind Hercules' eyes. *That's it*, he thought. *That's the answer!*

"Kill him," Ferocius said.

5

"No!" Hercules shouted. "Listen to me!" But six of Ferocius' guardsmen were rushing toward him, their dagger tips pointing at his eyes.

With one sweep of an arm, Hercules pushed Salmoneus behind him. "Get out of here!" he yelled over his shoulder.

"I don't think that's going to be so easy, Herc," Salmoneus answered. Hercules turned to see what Salmoneus was talking about. He saw a line of Ferocius' six other guardsmen, spears at the ready, charging the two of them.

Caught between two lines of onrushing soldiers, Salmoneus ducked. He dived to the ground to avoid the lances.

The spearmen tripped over him, hitting the ground in a snarl of arms, legs, and sharp points.

Hercules turned to the row of daggermen and grabbed the soldier on the end of the line. Holding the man's wrist, Hercules swung him into his fellow soldiers, knocking them to the ground.

Behind Hercules, the spearmen jammed their lances into his back. Grunting in pain, he reached behind himself and pulled out the lances. Seeing him occupied, the daggermen thrust their blades up at Hercules' face.

Before the blades could touch him, Hercules whipped the lances around and across like a thresher cutting wheat and slammed them into the daggermen's hands. The blow sent the knives sailing into the woods as the men shouted in sudden pain.

From his many battles, Hercules knew that soldiers disarmed in the face of a powerful enemy usually pull out of battle in order to rearm or plan new tactics. He did not expect the Mercantilians to attack.

From front and back, they piled atop him. From other sides came other soldiers, adding their weight to that of Ferocius' guards.

The men pinned Hercules to the ground. A chain-mailed fist plunged at his jaw, ripping flesh from his chin. Hercules winced.

The fist struck again, slashing skin off his cheek. It grabbed the back of his head and shoved his face into the mud.

Salmoneus, still lying on the ground to remain as inconspicuous as possible, watched the pile of men shake and twitch as Hercules tried to shove them off. More men pounded onto each other—but suddenly, the pile went still. The only sound was the grunting, cursing, and muttering of things like "Get your elbow out of my ear" from the soldiers on the lower levels.

"Hercules!" Salmoneus shouted, terrified. He ran toward the stack of men.

Ferocius climbed to the top of the pile. "Don't let him up," he commanded. From his high perch, he looked around at the townspeople who had gathered to watch the spectacle. "Honorius!" he shouted. "Get up here. And you, fat man! You, Peuris—you get up here, too. We're going to pile onto this traitor until we crack every bone in his body."

"Gonna crack mine, too," a soldier on a lower layer muttered. The townspeople reluctantly began to climb the tower of bodies.

Like a geyser blast, soldiers were thrown into the air. With arms and legs flailing, they traced wide arcs in all directions before slamming into the ground.

The townspeople backed away in a wide circle. In the center of the circle stood the man the soldiers were trying to kill.

"Herc, you did it!" Salmoneus exulted.

But the demigod had only stunned them. The soldiers came howling back, with the cadets as reinforcements. General Ferocius was leading the charge personally, with Honorius running at his side.

Swinging swords and lances and daggers, three dozen cadets and soldiers hacked away. One of the daggers sliced into Hercules' leg; the soldier wielding it shoved it in deep and twisted it wildly. Another sliced his back, leaving a long, red welt as yet another pulled Hercules' hair so hard that his eyes teared up.

I'm in trouble, he thought. Too many swords and

spears and lances and daggers were coming at him all at once. One lucky slash would lay him out cold; another would kill him.

A face suddenly pushed at him. He recognized it: Peuris, slashing at him with mad fury. "Kill you! Kill you! Kill you!" the boy was screaming. Hercules ducked the boy's dagger, but it came chopping toward him again. "Kill you!"

A long, heavy sword swung down toward Hercules' neck. As it sliced through the air, he realized that it was going to miss him and hit Peuris, cutting off the boy's head.

As someone punched Hercules in the belly, he raised a hand and caught the oncoming sword. Its blade sliced into the wedge of flesh between his thumb and index finger, and the pain was so great that he felt he might black out.

One of the soldiers in the melee turned and faced the others. He whipped his sword through the air over Hercules. It swept from side to side, knocking lances and spears to the ground, shielding the demigod from attack.

"Stop this!" the sword wielder shouted. It was the voice of Honorius.

The soldiers, accustomed to obeying their captain, obeyed. Their let their weapons drop to their sides.

"What's going on?" Hercules asked. He was startled to hear the same words come from Ferocius.

The general stood at the front of the crowd of soldiers and pointed his bloody sword tip at Honorius. "Answer me," he ordered.

"This man saved my son's life," Honorius said.

"A sword—your sword, general—was going to be-head my boy. But Hercules stopped it. He risked in-jury and death to save a cadet who—I'm sorry, son—wanted to kill him.

"I think we've misjudged him."

Ferocius did not lower his sword. "And I think he's a traitor. Men, here are your orders—"

"I've got an idea," said Salmoneus.

The peddler had placed himself at the edge of the crowd of soldiers, out of danger. Prevented from es-cape by his concern for Hercules (and by a crowd of housewives who surrounded him and refused to let him leave), he had observed the entire affair. Now, he shouldered through the crowd and allowed himself a dramatic pause.

"Get on with it," Ferocius commanded. *Yes, please*, Hercules thought. *I appreciate the help, but I'm bleeding here.*

With a smug smile, Salmoneus began: "It's simple, really. You're concerned that Hercules is a traitor. On the other hand, he's proved by saving the boy's life that he's got some wonderful qualities. Is he good, or is he bad? You feel that there's evidence on both sides. So you need a tiebreaker. Why not give him one? Give him a chance to show that he's really a great guy and on your side. And I mean a show of his true valor, not just a test of strength like that bit with the fake boulder or throwing your soldiers into the air."

Honorius spoke up. "Sounds reasonable. General, what do you think?"

Ferocius cupped his bearded chin in his hand and

41

looked annoyed. The smooth talker did indeed sound reasonable.

Ferocious didn't like reasonable people. They distracted soldiers by making them think that everyone had a sensible viewpoint, even the enemy. That sort of thing weakened their resolve and allowed the enemy to defeat them.

Still, he knew that he couldn't oppose something that sounded reasonable. Doing so would only make him sound crazy. Soldiers didn't like to follow crazy commanders.

Ferocius smiled. "Very well. Let him prove himself. Hercules—or whatever your true name is—since you destroyed our boulder weapon, I want you to go into Pastoralis and bring back *their* most valuable weapon. And do it by tomorrow night. I've heard that they plan to attack at the following dawn, and I want their weapon in my hands well before then."

Hercules considered the idea. It seemed fair, if dangerous.

Moreover, he thought, retrieving a dangerous weapon seemed a good first step to stopping a war. In any case, he'd have to enter Pastoralis and deal with the people there anyhow. Maybe if he could prove himself to both sides, he could bring them to the negotiating table.

He pulled himself up to his full height, which hurt his wounded leg. "Very well," he said, offering a hand for Ferocius to shake. "I'll get the weapon. Mind telling me what it is?"

Ferocius shook Hercules' hand. "Not at all," he

said. Blood from Hercules' wounded hand had flowed onto Ferocius'; he wiped it onto his breastplate.

Ferocius grinned. "It's the head of General Slaughterius, the Pastoralians' leader."

6

"Now, wait just a minute," Hercules protested. "I'm not bringing back anyone's head."

Ferocius stared at the demigod and realized that he wasn't bluffing. "Very well. Officers, enlisted soldiers, cadets—on my command. . . ." With crisp, synchronized precision, the soldiers raised their sharpest weapons and pointed them at a big, broad target: Hercules' chest.

Hercules clenched his fists and tensed his shoulders, bracing himself for another battle. He bent his knees slightly to find out how agile and flexible he was, and didn't like the answer. *I can't run far or fast with the wound in my leg. Can't leap out of the way. I'll have to stand and fight. I just wish my hand didn't hurt so much.*

"Ready . . . aim . . ."

"Gentlemen, gentlemen, *gentle*men," Salmoneus said soothingly, elbowing through soldiers on his way to Hercules and Ferocius. "You mustn't kill this man. After all, when you're done, you'll probably want to kill me, because I'm his friend, even though I've done nothing to offend you, have I?"

"You're getting pretty close to it," Ferocius growled.

"Ah, yes," Salmoneus said. He went on quickly: "In any event, there's an easy way to fix this situation. Don't kill Hercules. Send him to the Pastoralians with whatever orders you want—except bringing back someone's head—and send someone to monitor him and make sure he carries out the orders. Simple, no?"

Ferocius bit his lip. He didn't like the idea of letting the traitor leave his sight—yet obviously this fellow wouldn't go quietly, and the prospect of another battle as fierce as the one his men had just fought did not please him. There was no guarantee that they would win. Their opponent clearly had strength beyond that of normal men. Besides, the fight had tired his soldiers, and he'd need them fresh to fight the Pastoralians.

On the other hand, this Salmoneus' plan was flawed. Ferocius didn't like to send his men on hopeless missions—and sending one to help a traitor infiltrate the enemy camp on the eve of a major battle, with orders to kill the enemy commander, was a recipe for suicide. Ideally, the enemy soldiers would kill this Hercules impostor, saving Ferocius the trouble.

If only there was someone else to send with him, someone expendable.

"You," Ferocius said to Salmoneus, "you go with him and monitor him."

"Me?" Salmoneus backed into the hard breastplate of a large, scowling soldier. "No, no. See, I had planned to stay here and soak up the local color. You know, customs, manners, life in your little town, a few chats with your lovely ladies, that sort of thing. I'm a businessman, not a fighter. One of your big, brawny hulks here would be much better than me. This one, for instance," he looked up at the huge man he'd bumped into. "He'd be a fine candidate." The soldier snarled at him. "Well," Salmoneus went on, "maybe not him, but any number of these other excellent soldiers would—"

"You," Ferocius repeated, "you go with him. And if he's not back here by tomorrow night with Slaughterius' head, then my soldiers will attack Slaughterius' city the next morning—and we'll be looking for you."

Salmoneus gulped. Hercules gave his shoulder a pat meant to be reassuring; Salmoneus jumped as if a lightning bolt had hit him.

"All right, everyone, show's over," Honorius shouted. "Back to your homes. Soldiers, officers, and cadets, back to your barracks. Get moving."

He turned to Hercules and Salmoneus. "Come with me. I'll find you a place to rest and get you some ointments and bandages for those wounds."

He settled them in a hut with walls and roof of yellowed, woven reeds. Inside were a wooden table with warped planks, and a bench of rocks held together with mud. A straw mat lay on the ground. Moonlight filtered through the gaps in the peaked reed ceiling.

"Sorry about the condition of the place," Honorius said. "We haven't had the money to fix any of the buildings."

He pointed out the doorway at a cylinder poking through the ground near the spot where the fake boulder had stood. "You can get water from the well in the center of town. Food—well, I'll see if I can get you something in the morning. And don't bother trying to escape; the town's entrance is well guarded. Good night."

He left. For a moment, there was silence.

Salmoneus broke it. "Well, this is just great," he griped as he lay on the straw mat. "You have to kill a man, and I have to help, or die."

"Relax, Salmoneus," Hercules said, rubbing his back. The pain from his scrapes and welts was dizzying. Noise from his traveling companion made it worse.

"I will not relax!" Salmoneus whined. He sat straight up. "We've got to get out of here. These people think you're a traitor, and only Olympus knows what they think of me. They don't even *want* your help. Look, I don't want them to go to war, either, but it's their choice. Why not let them live their own lives?"

"It's not their choice, Salmoneus," Hercules said. "A god is using them. Whoever he is, I can't just let him wipe them out."

"Why?" Salmoneus screeched. "Why, just this once, can't you worry about your own life?" He lay down on the mat again. "You're going to get us both hacked to bits, you know. I'll bet the only thing that could make you happier is if someone were lurking around this hut, waiting to kill us."

"Someone is," Hercules said softly.

"What?" Salmoneus shouted. "Are you insane? Hercules, you have to protect me. I swear, I haven't been in such trouble since—" Hercules clamped a hand over his mouth.

"Shh," Hercules whispered. "Over your shoulder, through the slits between the reeds in the wall, I saw someone moving. He's near the doorway now. We could be in danger."

He let go of his friend's face. "Move around. Make noise. Distract him."

Salmoneus began a steady stream of loud chatter. As he shouted and pounded the wooden table, Hercules crept to the door.

Hercules pounced. He found himself grabbing a whirlwind of pinwheeling arms and kicking legs, plus a mouth screaming like a trapped sparrow.

He grabbed his quarry's head and pulled it back to see his prisoner's face. "I don't want to hurt you, but if you don't knock off the noise, I'll—Peuris!"

Salmoneus poked his head out of the hut. "What's *he* doing here?"

"I just—" Honorius came up behind him. Hercules let him go; the boy ran to his father.

His face filled with dark anger, Honorius demanded of Hercules, "Why are you hurting my son?"

"He didn't hurt me, Dad," Peuris said. More townspeople were gathering. The boy, embarrassed, looked at his feet. "It's . . . it's my fault. I was hanging around to find out what he'd say on his own, away from us. I thought . . . well, I didn't like him, but then he saved my life, and . . . I was confused. I had to know what he really thought. You know, about us and the war."

The boy looked up at Hercules. "I'm sorry. You're all right." He looked around at the dozens of faces staring at him, then suddenly turned and ran.

Honorius started after him. He looked back at Hercules for a moment. "Thanks," he said, and turned to catch up with his son.

The crowd slowly dispersed. Hercules watched Honorius hug his boy and speak softly to him.

"That's what makes these people worth helping, Salmoneus. If they can see something good in someone they think is a traitor—"

But he was talking to himself. Salmoneus had already gone inside.

Hercules entered the hut and found Salmoneus snoring on the mat. *Well, it's the floor for me.* He fingered the wounds on his leg and back, and sighed. "Pleasant dreams, Salmoneus." He groaned as he lowered himself to the hard, cold ground.

Hercules stared at the ceiling. *Tomorrow,* he thought, *we really get in trouble.*

7

The sunrise spread a buttery glow over the dusty streets and reed buildings of Mercantilius. The light slid from the city into the forest, bathing a million leaves in tawny light and drawing long bars of tree shadows on the dewy grass.

The forest sloped up to a high ridge. On the other side, the trees at the bottom lay cool in the ridge's shadow. Beyond the trees stood a tall, white wall, the sunlight painting it yellow.

Quarried from thick sheets of granite, the wall stood ninety feet high and three hundred feet long. Two men—one grumbling, the other nauseatingly pleased with himself—were climbing a ladder carved into the wall's face.

Salmoneus, the smaller of the two men, climbed quickly as a monkey. He was whistling and proud in garish finery: a silken toga of the purest silver, tied with a belt of sky-blue satin with gold embroidery. He had shampooed, creamed, and brushed his hair until it shone like the sleekest mink. On his head lay a crown of sweet bay and cherry laurel leaves. His fingers displayed a heavy load of rings painted to look like polished gold; about his neck hung several sparkling pendants and flashing medallions. His overall appearance was gaudy, florid, vulgar, and tasteless.

He loved it.

Behind him, Hercules glanced up and muttered, "You look like a fairground decorated for a three-day carnival."

"Why, thank you, Hercules." Salmoneus, quite pleased, practically sang the words. "And I thought you didn't like this outfit. Of course," he went on with a sympathetic smile, "it certainly beats yours."

It certainly did. Salmoneus had risen before dawn to gather the materials for what he called his masterpiece. He had taken scraps and ribbons of cast-off colored fabric—screaming orange, runny-snot green, blinding pink, muddy gray, shrieking sunburst yellow, and a wavy pattern of red-purple swirls that upset the stomach of almost anyone who looked at it—and formed them into a makeshift sack. Cutting holes in the sack for legs, arms, and a head, Salmoneus had pronounced the suit perfect.

He had helped Hercules maneuver himself into the baggy outfit, slapped a pair of long, flat sandals on his feet, painted his hands and face white as marble, glued a tiny red ball to his nose, and, as a finishing touch, cut the tail half off a roan stallion and knotted it to Hercules' hair as a wig.

Although Hercules had objected to Salmoneus' work, he had no better plan. He had spent the night recovering from his wounds and trying fitfully to get enough sleep for the next day's exertions. Consequently, he'd had little energy for dreaming up a clever scheme that would satisfy Ferocius without actually beheading the leader of the Pastoralians.

The work was going to be more difficult than he had first thought. Honorius had dropped by just before they left town and offered some advice.

No one knew much about the Pastoralians' city, he had said. It was protected by enormous walls that formed a barrier around the city and hid it from outsiders.

In the past, Honorius had said, the few visitors who had gone inside the walls had called the city-state a gentle, quiet land, as befitted a town of shepherds and herdsmen. Since hostilities had risen between Mercantilius and Pastoralis, though, rumors had spread that the Pastoralians had turned military. All of the citizens were armed and drilling for battle, including women and children; Pastoralian researchers were devising catapults that could fire a dozen boulders per minute; and every morning, all citizens were required to shout out curses and threats directed at Mercantilius, stoking their anger for the war to come. And they did not like strangers.

What's more, their General Slaughterius was a monster. He had personally commanded all of these changes and imprisoned anyone who opposed him.

He actually enjoyed killing; he had executed many prisoners personally. Or so, said Honorius, the rumors reported.

Now, slipping up a sheer wall in a clown suit, Hercules concentrated on dreaming up two plans: one to head off the war and the other to punish Salmoneus. Just as he began to envision coating Salmoneus in fish sauce and dipping him into a vat of hungry ducks, the peddler spoke up.

"Don't look now, Herc," Salmoneus whispered, "but it's showtime."

Hercules looked up. Althought they were only a third of the way up the wall, they had reached the top of the ladder. Next to the ladder, carved into the wall, ran a long, deep walkway. According to Honorius, each wall had the same ladder-and-walkway arrangement.

The city's leaders had placed the great stone walls so that they did not quite meet, leaving a gap at each corner. Only at these corners could anyone enter the city.

Hercules and Salmoneus moved along the walkway toward the nearest corner. Hercules peered forward; at the corner, he could see a round, railed-off platform. On it stood four guards wearing gleaming body armor and carrying pointed clubs.

Each guard had specialized his weapon. One man's club bristled with jagged iron spikes. The guard next to him was sanding down his club to a slick finish, to make it fly smoothly through the air when thrown; it was tied to his wrist with a long leather strap for easy retrieval. The third guard was painting his club with a gluey fluid whose sickly-sweet aroma Hercules recognized. Waving the fluid through the air would set it on fire, making the club extra deadly.

The burliest guard wore a blue sash from shoulder to hip. Clearly, he was the commander. He carried a club covered in granite chunks to rip the flesh off his victims.

Led by Salmoneus, Hercules moved along the walkway, his long sandals flapping. Only a thin railing kept them from falling and hitting the ground with a wet splat.

As they neared the guard station, Hercules looked down at his slapshoes and the shapeless outfit that he'd started to think of as a rainbow bladder. "This," grumbled the world's strongest man, "is the stupidest plan I've ever been involved with."

"Nonsense. It's brilliant," Salmoneus whispered. "I don't care how touchy these guys are, no one ever suspects a clown. Let's go."

With a straight back and puffed-out chest, Salmoneus burst from the walkway and into the guard station like the star of a sold-out recital presenting himself to an eager crowd. His arms outstretched, his back arched, his face beaming, Salmoneus simply stood for a moment and let the guards absorb his presence.

The guards raised their weapons but waited for Salmoneus to declare himself friend or foe. "Ladies and gent—I mean, gentlemen and, uh, gentlemen," the peddler-turned-showman declared, "I have come to bring you entertainment. On the orders of General Slaughterius himself, I have come from the far corners of the civilized world, from Phrygia and Sumeria and Samarkand, yea, even from Cathay and Cipango, to present to you the one, the only, the incomparable . . . Goofius the Comedian!''

Hercules stepped forward, his shoes flapping on the walkway's floor. Salmoneus slipped behind him to give him room to perform.

The guards watched Hercules with stony skepticism. ''Hi, guys,'' he grumped, and waved a stiff, nearly lifeless hand.

He heard Salmoneus hissing in his ear. ''That's not how you do it,'' the peddler complained. ''Sell it! And for Olympus' sake, smile!''

''I told you when you were sewing me into this getup, I'm not good at this stuff,'' Hercules muttered through a gritted-teeth grin.

''Just sing your song,'' Salmoneus urged. He gave Hercules a push; ordinarily, the shove wouldn't have moved him an inch, but the slapshoes on his feet unbalanced him. The big man stumbled forward and landed face first on the guard platform's floor. He turned to glare at Salmoneus.

The guards laughed.

Hercules stared at them, amazed. *They like me? Really?* He looked back at Salmoneus, who nodding vigorously and was waving him forward, encouraging him toward the guards.

Hercules turned toward them. They were watching him, waiting for more pratfalls. The burly commander with the granite club crossed his arms. ''Well?'' he asked in a gruff, heavy tone. ''Was that all?'' The guards' smiles faded.

"That," Hercules improvised, standing and brushing himself off, "was, uh, just a sample of the entertainment that awaits the great Slaughterius. But the rest of the show is reserved for him alone."

"Right!" Salmoneus declared, bounding past Hercules. He looked up at the chief guard. "We have heard that his heart is heavy and his mind is weary from planning battles, and thus we have come to lighten his load so that he may think and plan more easily, and thereby ensure victory for all of Pastoralis."

"Right," Hercules said. "Take us to him."

The guards huddled. Salmoneus leaned forward and cocked an ear to eavesdrop on their conference, but Hercules pulled him back. "Don't be rude," he whispered. "It could get you killed."

The huddle broke up. The guard with the spiked club sprinted into the city as the commander stepped forward.

"He's going to General Slaughterius' quarters," the man barked. "We didn't hear you were coming, but the boss might have secrets we don't know about."

He stared at the two men for a long moment. Salmoneus pulled at the neck of his toga, as if it suddenly was too tight. He grinned meekly at the brute in the blue sash; the man did not grin back. Glancing nervously at the men's muscles, weapons, and grim faces, Salmoneus stayed close to Hercules.

He let out a sigh of relief when the sprinter came dashing back with four other guards behind him. The sprinter nodded at his commander. "All right," said the commander. "You're in." He pointed his club at Hercules and Salmoneus. "Positions, men."

The guards who had been on the platform assembled themselves into the points of a triangle around their guests, two behind Hercules and Salmoneus and one in front. They kept their clubs trained on the prisoners.

The commander set off between the towering stone walls, and the soldiers behind Hercules and Salmoneus began marching. Taking their cue, Hercules and Salmoneus fell into step. The four remaining guards stayed behind.

Hercules muttered to Salmoneus, "Brace yourself. Remember, these people are supposed to be military fanatics. We're sticking our heads in the lion's mouth now." *And I've got to protect both of us,* he thought.

The walls were thick, studded with thousands of small stones and pebbles. Rising high on both sides, they formed a long corridor that blocked out the sunlight. A chilly wind blew, disturbing the hair on Hercules' arms and legs, and making him itch.

Hercules noticed Salmoneus shivering and wished that he had an animal skin to lend him—then realized that Salmoneus was shivering in fear. The big guard with the raspy club kept swinging his weapon back and forth while staring at the two men.

At last, descending a stairway, they approached a tall sliver of light: the morning sunlight slipping between the walls up ahead. Hercules had no doubt that the gap led into the city.

Here it comes, Hercules thought. *The city of killers*

and warriors. Get ready for anything. He took a deep breath and tightened his fists.

They emerged into the light and caught their first view of Pastoralis. Hercules blinked; Salmoneus gaped.

They looked at each other and chorused, "Are you seeing what I'm—?" They stopped and turned back to stare at the city.

Before them stretched an immaculate lawn with a checkerboard pattern, squares of blue-green and yellow-green grasses that waved in a light breeze. The morning sunshine seemed cleaner than in the forest, making the dew on the grass sparkle like a field of diamonds. A sweet perfume, like roses and honeysuckle, eased gently through the air and drifted over Hercules and Salmoneus.

A flock of bluebirds swooped over the grass and settled atop one of the city's walls. A butterfly danced through the air, flapped toward Hercules and Salmoneus, and settled on Hercules' wrist. "It likes you," Salmoneus said as the creature fluttered away.

Hercules and Salmoneus were reluctant to go further. They felt soiled, heavy, and crude, like oxen in a temple. Their vulgar clothes and sweaty skin didn't belong in a place that seemed as light and pure as a rainbow.

In the distance stood a curving band of trees so perfectly pruned and shaped that they looked like giant dandelions. Behind them rose a semicircle of tall, thin buildings colored lavender and pastel pink and powder blue. Open and airy, with long, curved shapes, the buildings swept upward and pointed toward the cloudless, crystal-blue sky. One tower reminded Hercules of the graceful, upstretched arm of a dancer he once knew; another looked like the long, strong stem of a bird-of-paradise.

Were these impossibly elegant buildings homes, museums, or something else? Hercules had no idea. "Nice lion's mouth we're in," Salmoneus muttered.

Hercules scanned the view. "Notice something?" he asked Salmoneus. "No people." To the soldiers he said, "Where is everyone?"

The soldier with the granite club and blue sash grunted. "Ambitius warned everyone we were bringing in outsiders. They're probably waiting for an all-clear sign."

He pressed a finger onto the tip of his club. To Hercules' surprise, the finger sank in easily. The club popped open, splitting neatly in two halves held together by a thin strip of calfskin. Within the club, someone had hollowed out a curving groove. In the groove lay a thin, long horn.

The commander pulled the horn out of the club and raised it to his lips. He produced a blast lasting a solid minute at surprisingly high volume.

As he blew, heads began to pop out of some of the nearer buildings: beautiful, female heads connected to beautiful, female bodies. The women whirled and cavorted over the checkerboard lawn. The dancers were slim as the towers, with strong legs tapering to delicate ankles. They wore filmy wisps of nothing much, which fluttered about them as they spun and pranced. Their hair cascaded down their backs in shining streams; their skin was pink and bright; their smiling teeth, brilliantly white.

"Salmoneus," Hercules said, "close your mouth. You're drooling." Salmoneus didn't respond. Hercules gently slid his index finger under Salmoneus' jaw and pushed his sagging chin up until his lower teeth clicked lightly against his uppers.

Salmoneus slapped his own cheek and winced at the pain. "Well," he said, "I'm not dreaming and I'm not dead. Looks like Honorius lied to us about how rough this place is."

"I don't think so," Hercules mused. "He would have known we'd find the truth out as soon as we—"

"He treated us like easy marks," Salmoneus said, shock stealing over his face. "Like tourists to be fleeced, like—like we were his *customers!*" To Salmoneus, the expert salesman, the thought that someone could treat him like a common sucker buying souvenirs in a bazaar was distasteful. He spat.

"Well," he went on, "that's that. Let's go over to the side of these people. They seem nice and—" a lithe, blonde dancer gamboled by and smiled at Salmoneus—"friendly."

"I'm not so sure," Hercules said. "Honorius doesn't seem like the lying type. He must have heard some false rumors about this place and just passed them on to us."

"Who cares?" Salmoneus said. The blonde dancer pulled a strip of gauzy, sparkling fabric from her blouse, revealing a firm midriff, and laid it around Salmoneus' neck. She tickled him under the chin and leaped away, blowing him a kiss.

"Forget Jayos Lenodiis and the lecture circuit," he went on. "I'm going to set up shop right here. Sell a few beads and trinkets to these lovely ladies—" He pulled one of the medallions off his neck and tossed it in the direction of the blonde dancer; without interrupting the flow of her dance, she bent down to pick it up and tossed it into the air, catching it with one slim hand.

"Free introductory sample, to get them talking about the new line of merchandise," Salmoneus explained.

"Don't build dream castles," Hercules said. "You—uh-oh!"

"Uh-oh? What do you mean by 'uh'. . . . Oh."

From the largest building in sight, a man and a woman strode toward Hercules and Salmoneus. As they passed, the dancers bent their legs and, like dying swans, slowly sank downward in low curtseys. The guards surrounding the men knelt, tilting their heads toward the ground and laying their weapons flat on the grass in a gesture of deference.

Hercules and Salmoneus were the only ones standing. Hercules felt as exposed as a black cat on a field of snow.

"Do we kneel?" Salmoneus asked him.

"Absolutely not," the big man answered. "We're not their subjects. Just be careful."

"Sssh! They're stopping."

The man was tall and very thin, his skin pale as paper. He appeared to be in his fifties, or older. His wispy hair was the color of sand, and thinning; he had brushed his remaining hair forward to hide the loss, but it was too fine and sparse to conceal anything. His eyes were a watery gray, and the skin at their edges curved downward, giving him a melancholy look.

He sniffled. With slim, spidery fingers, he pulled a handkerchief from within his shimmering purple toga and wiped his long nose. His legs reminded Hercules of a rooster his mother had raised. It was a scrawny thing, too stringy to eat, and its legs were as bony and angular as those of the man before him.

Despite the man's gangly frame, his belly was going to fat. His silhouette was that of a toothpick with a pea stuck onto its middle. Hercules had seen stronger-looking skeletons.

"Why, hello," the man said in a voice so high and quiet that Salmoneus thought for a moment that the woman had spoken. The man held out a limp hand. His arms were extraordinarily long—his hands reached nearly to his knees. "I am Slaughterius, the leader of this humble little community. Do forgive me for using such a ferocious-looking guard, but they're only there to scare away people who might *hurt* my gentle kingdom."

So much for the macho monster Honorius said this guy was, Hercules thought. But there was no time for musing; Salmoneus was talking.

"Greetings, your majesty! I am Salmoneus, agent for the talented, producer of the miraculous, creator of entertainments famed throughout a dozen nations and too many city-states to number. The great oaf at my side is Goofius the Fool, clown extraordinaire. His buffoonish antics and childish silliness are sure to delight and amuse you, as they have the crowned heads of Assyria, Mesopotamia, Babylonia, and the Persian Empire. Why, I have seen him plummet from the nose of the Sphinx in Egypt, tumble downward through the air for the span of a hundred heartbeats, pick up speed every instant, land with a splat loud enough to wake your dead grandmother, and bounce to his feet as if he'd simply rolled out of bed . . . a stunt that he will happily duplicate for you this very day." Salmoneus paused; a thought struck him. "But why merely duplicate it? He will, if you wish, actually outdo it!"

Salmoneus, Hercules thought, *what are you getting me into?*

Like many a salesman, Salmoneus was getting carried away by the sound of his own voice and making exaggerated promises to land a client. He may even have believed them.

Fortunately, Slaughterius stopped him. "Thank you, my dear boy," he said mildly. He gestured to the woman accompanying him. She was tall and blonde, with blazing blue eyes. "And this lady is my dear, darling friend and ally—"

"Dryope," Hercules realized, recognizing her. He immediately regretted saying the name. His ridiculous makeup and outfit might hide his appearance, but what if she should recognize his voice?

She peered at him curiously. "Do I know you?" she asked. She leaned toward him and gazed into his eyes. "You do look familiar. . . ."

"But of course!" Salmoneus shouted, sliding between the two demigods. "Goofius is celebrated throughout the Greek Isles! Audiences from Atlantis to Scandahoovia have laughed themselves sick over his magnificently dopey face with its stupid expressions and imbecilic features." He grabbed Hercules by the jaw and yanked it forward. "Tell me, madam, is this not the face of a complete and total goon?"

I'll get you for this, Salmoneus, Hercules thought.

"Mmmm. . . ." Dryope mused. "I suppose you're right." Salmoneus released Hercules' jaw; Hercules rubbed it to ease out the pain and shot a sidelong, angry glance at his friend.

Dryope turned to Slaughterius. "My dear," she purred as she slipped her arm into his, "can you offer our new friends lodging? They seem to have traveled far, and no doubt they need to rest from their journey."

She ran her fingers up the back of his neck and tickled the tiny wisps of curly hair between his ears. Slaughterius smiled at her. "A fine idea, my dear," he said, giving her a quick kiss on the nose.

Hercules tried not to grimace. *Dryope, you're at it again,* he thought. He felt tired. *Don't enrapture the mortals. Leave them alone, for Zeus' sake.*

Slaughterius and Dryope turned and ambled back toward one of the slim, curving towers. "Oh, Captain *Vicius*," Slaughterius sang out.

The burly commander galloped up to his leader. "Yes, sire?"

"Give our guests a place to stay and some food and wine," Slaughterius said in a languid, uncaring tone. "They will perform tomorrow at noon."

"Noon?" asked Salmoneus. "But don't you have

something important tomorrow at dawn?''

Hercules held back his shock. *Salmoneus, you talk too much. If they ask how you know they're doing something important at dawn, that gives away our whole mission!*

"Why, yes," Slaughterius told Salmoneus without turning around. "We're going to butcher quite a number of—well, I suppose I should call them beasts."

Beasts, Hercules thought. *That's what they think of the Mercantilians. Ferocius was right about one thing—they really are planning an attack at dawn.*

"We've been having *such* trouble selling our cows and sheep—someone has been spreading disgraceful rumors that they're not healthy to eat—that we're going to butcher them ourselves, cook them, and eat them in public to show that they're safe," Slaughterius went on. "We've invited the leaders of *all* the local city-states—except those *dreadful* Mercantilians, of course. Rumors, rumors, rumors—they're just awful for business, aren't they? Well, we're going to get rid of them once and for all. Good day, everyone." And he and Dryope swept away.

Hercules watched them go, but his mind was elsewhere. *If I don't bring back Slaughterius's head tonight, the Mercs'll attack tomorrow morning. And when they do, they'll massacre these people—and all the leaders from the other towns. The people in those towns are going to want revenge. They'll attack the Mercantilians. The Mercs'll counterattack. The other towns will fight back. Endless war.*

He swept his eyes over the shimmering towers and imagined them scorched by flames. He looked at the peaceful, green meadow before him, covered with young girls carelessly sunning themselves, and envisioned a ravaged field covered with stabbed and broken bodies.

Well, now I know who my enemy is, he thought. *I should have guessed who it was. That guy who was laughing in the dark last night—I should have known. He laughs at war all the time. He loves it.*

"Ares," he said. *My own half brother.*

8

"Shh!" Salmoneus said, laying an angry finger over Hercules' lips. "You're supposed to be a dopey clown. Don't say anything even close to intelligent."

"Come this way," the soldier Vicius said. He and his men, still arranged in a triangle around Hercules and Salmoneus, marched forward, pushing their prisoners. Hercules and Salmoneus matched their pace, and the group strode down a sweeping pathway covered in shiny gravel. No, not exactly gravel, Hercules realized; the pebbles beneath their sandals were chips of glimmering opal.

The soldiers escorted their guests to a long building on the far end of the semicircle of dandelion trees and fairy-tale towers. The building, resting on a soft lawn, was a canopy of pink marble, thin as parchment. It curved upward from the ground to a high point and swooped back down to the lawn, like a circus tent. White marble pegs secured the "tent" to the grass.

Hercules and Salmoneus entered through a curtained hole in the marble. The doorway was shaped exactly like the building. Its gauzy drape was a rich purple, a dye found only in the faraway nation of Tyre. Light breezes slipped though the curtain.

Hercules gazed around the building and saw no flaw in its design or construction—no place where a sculptor's chisel slipped, no ugly sags, no rough edges. In all of his travels, he had rarely seen a building that so perfectly merged delicate beauty with complete practicality.

The building covered a space so long and wide that gladiators could fight lions there. Freestanding, hinged partitions, hewn from cherrywood and polished to a high gleam, divided it into sections. For beauty of craftsmanship, Hercules thought, the elaborately carved partitions could surpass anything in the grand palaces of the Pharaoh in Egypt or the Emperor in Persia.

"Ahh," said Salmoneus, and settled snugly on one of the many brightly colored pillows that lay on the teakwood floor. He lay back and wiggled his bruised bottom into the velvety fabric.

"Thank you, boys," Salmoneus said, and waved the soldiers away with the back of his hand. "That will do. Oh, and do send over some food and drink for us. I would prefer some kippered pheasant's tongue, lightly spiced cabbage—and none of that cheap Carthaginian cabbage, either; only the good

Cretan stuff—some of your finest wine from the Champagne region of Gaul, and for dessert, cakes with cinnamon and pies with chicory. Oh, and bring some food for my clown, too." He clapped his hands twice, briskly. "Go, now. And be quick about it."

The soldiers tromped out, grumbling. Salmoneus leaned back and stretched like a fat, yawning panther. Sunlight warmed his face. The top of the building was not solid but a screenlike mesh of needle-thin, interlacing marble rods that would let in light but blocked insects. "Ahhh," the peddler sighed. "Now this, as the sages say, is the life."

Hercules picked him up, not too roughly. "And you, as the sages say, are nuts," he said quietly. "In case you've forgotten, we're here to stop a war, not indulge your taste for luxury."

Salmoneus carefully peeled Hercules' fingers from his shoulders. "Now, now, Herc, relax. I know what we're here for. But no one says we can't enjoy ourselves as we go. Besides, these people aren't warlike."

"I know," Hercules said quietly. In even lower tones, he went on, "That king of theirs couldn't fight a war even if you gave him Zeus's own lightning bolts and the speed of Hermes." He sat on a pillow, then pulled it out from under him and sat on the floor. "I think he and his people are going to be slaughtered. No pun intended.

"Ares set this whole thing up to start not just one war, but a whole batch of them." Hercules scratched the back of his neck thoughtfully and remembered one of the war god's first experiments with battle, a skirmish that became a feud that blew up into a decade-long series of bloody fights all over the Middle East.

"He'll just sit back on Olympus and laugh as people die." As a boy, Hercules had been shocked to witness one of Ares' early experiments in mass death: an ambush that wounded a hundred innocents fatally. When a hundred more rushed in to rescue them, the rescuers died as well. Ares had rocked back and forth, guffawing until he was nearly breathless.

"How do you know he's behind this?" Salmoneus asked, pulling a green satin pillow under his head.

"I don't know for certain," Hercules admitted. "But all of the facts point at him. There's only one way to stop his plan. We've got to tell the Mercantilians not to attack at dawn, or any other time."

Salmoneus leaned toward Hercules and spoke so softly that Hercules had to strain to hear his voice. "How're we going to do that? In case you didn't notice, the only ways out of this town are at the corners between the walls, and the guards at those corners are pretty quick with the clubs."

"I know," Hercules whispered. "Let's work out a plan." He arranged four pillows in a square on the floor. "Let's say that these pillows are the walls."

He glanced out the doorway and noticed knobby, sandaled feet marching back and forth, guarding the two from unnecessary interruption—or perhaps preventing them from leaving before their performance. He continued planning in a voice quieter than a cat on tiptoe as their guard went back and forth.

9

There was no moon that night. Clouds hid the stars. It was only nine o'clock, yet the city was as dark as the inside of a dog.

Hercules stood with his back pressed against the inner wall of the marble tent, an inch from the doorway. Dressed in his customary shirt and pants (which he had tucked inside the clown suit), he listened hard.

He heard only the footsteps of the guard, crunching back and forth on the gravel path. Hercules glanced at Salmoneus, waiting on the other side of the doorway in his fancy toga, and nodded. It was time to get to work. Salmoneus gulped.

Slowly, Hercules reached for the purple curtain covering the doorway, and slipped his fingers around it. He whipped it aside with a rustling flurry, and let go.

The guard pivoted, drew his sword, and watched the drape quietly swing back and forth with no one near it. Obviously, no one had left the building. Whoever disturbed the drape must have gone inside.

Slowly the guard approached the doorway, tiptoeing so as not to let the intruder hear his footsteps. He clutched his club in one hand; with the other, he quietly pulled the drape aside.

A hand as large as a bull's head grabbed his fingers, crushing them together painfully, and pulled him forward. The drape, still in the guard's hands, ripped; Salmoneus winced at the sound, hoping no one would hear it. The guard stumbled but never dropped his club.

In the darkness within the building, the guard could not see the person who was grabbing him. He swung his club in a full circle, hoping to hit whomever was there.

Salmoneus, standing in front of the guard, backed away and tripped over a pillow. He went tumbling backward and cracked his head on the floor. He cursed.

The sound alerted the guard to Salmoneus' position. With a surge of strength, he wrenched himself free of the fist gripping his hand. He leaped, and smashed his club into a pillow lying between Salmoneus' legs.

Salmoneus screamed. He clapped his mouth shut—but his quick squeal was enough. The guard aimed his club at Salmoneus' throat and lunged.

But the huge hand grabbed the soldier around the

chest. It yanked him back as another beefy hand hit two quick chops to his neck.

The guard's head dropped back. His eyes rolled up, his eyelids closed, and he sagged like a sack of wet sand. Only Hercules' strong grip on his torso kept the guard from collapsing entirely and making an unwanted thump on the floor.

"You all right, Salmoneus?" Hercules whispered as he grabbed his friend's wrists and pulled him to his feet.

"Me? Sure. Wasn't even scared," Salmoneus lied. He wiped hot sweat off his forehead. "Thanks." To himself, he muttered, "Boy, what I do to make a few drachmas!"

"Come on," Hercules whispered, dropping Salmoneus' wrists. "We don't have much time." They slipped silently out of their lodgings and gingerly stepped across the opal pathway.

Although it seemed no one was watching them, Salmoneus grimaced at every twitch and rustle of the opal flakes under their sandals. Crossing the path, a distance as wide as a horse is long, seemed to take centuries.

Hercules looked over his shoulder and saw the terror in his friend's eyes, the shivering in his fingers, and the quick snap of his head from side to side at any tiny sound. He leaned back and wrapped an arm around Salmoneus' waist. As if the man were as light as a toenail, Hercules lifted him off the ground.

Hercules tucked the peddler under his armpit. Salmoneus' bottom was pointing at the sky and his arms were dangling toward the backs of Hercules' knees. *When this is all over*, Hercules thought, *I'm going to get Salmoneus on a diet. If I'm going to carry him around, he'd better lay off the heavy desserts.*

He raced lightly across the checkerboard lawn, looking for guards. One of them stood at the nearest gap between the city walls, but he was facing the gap, not the lawn. He didn't seem to notice Hercules.

Salmoneus' back twitched as if a puppeteer had pulled a string and jerked his head up. *Now what?* Hercules thought, and glanced down at Salmoneus. The smaller man was gaping at something behind Hercules. The big man turned to see what it was.

The grass was moving.

One of the checkerboard squares near their lodgings was not lying flat but was angling up like a trapdoor, as if its blue-green grasses had decided to sit up and face Hercules and Salmoneus.

The square, at least ten feet on each side, began to drop toward the ground, like some massive beast shutting its jaw. A thin wisp of a groan escaped from below the square.

Dropping Salmoneus, Hercules dashed to the square. He was too late. It had shut.

Hercules knelt to examine the square. It seemed to join up to the surrounding squares and flow into them without a seam or crack. As he ran his fingers along the edge of the square, he felt a whisper-thin gap. He couldn't see it, though; the long, wavy grasses hid it from view.

"What in the name of Zeus are you doing?" Salmoneus whispered. Hercules looked over his shoulder to find Salmoneus bending over him, outraged.

"Didn't you hear that moan? Someone under this thing is hurt." Hercules turned back to the checker-board square and tried to slip his fingers into the gap. "I'm going to help."

Salmoneus buried his face in his hands. "Aw, *no,*" he whined. "We were just about to get out of here."

"You go if you want," Hercules said. His fingers were too wide to fit into the gap. He slid his hands along the lawn, searching for a way to grip the elusive line. "I can't leave whoever it is down there."

Salmoneus glanced back at the massive walls, at the gap between them, and at the guard facing the gap. Watching him, Hercules felt he knew what was on the merchant's mind. He probably believed that he could sneak up on the guard and get past him by fast talking. Or even talk the guards into letting him leave the city. Or at least he could slip past and lose them in the darkness. He might be able to find his way off Peloponnesus, although that would be difficult. Ships didn't dock in a war zone if they could help it.

Hercules smiled to himself. His smile died as he looked over his shoulder and noticed the guard yawn-ing and stretching. *Don't turn around*, Hercules thought.

The guard seemed to spy something out of the cor-ner of his eye. *He's going to see us.*

Hercules caught sight of a horn dangling from a belt around the guard's waist. The horn was larger than the one that Captain Vicius had blown to an-nounce "all clear" when he had brought Hercules and Salmoneus in. *One blast from that pipe, and everyone in this town wakes up*, Hercules thought. *Once they find the guard I knocked out, they'll never let us out of here*.

The guard was beginning to turn around. It was time, Hercules decided, for fast action. He whispered, "Salmoneus—"

"Not now, Herc," the peddler complained, sliding his fingers through the gap between squares. "I think I've got something here."

"Excuse me," Hercules said. With one hand, he grabbed Salmoneus by the toga and pulled him aside. He shoved his other hand into the soft ground up to his wrist. With a rough yank, he ripped the green square out of the dirt.

As bits of the square's loose soil dripped onto his shoulders, Hercules hurled himself into the hole that lay beneath the square, pulling Salmoneus behind him with one hand and tugging the square into place atop the hole with the other hand. *If anyone sees anything wrong with how that square sits in the ground*, he thought, *we're dead*.

As the ground slipped away beneath them, he looked down. *On the other hand, we've got bigger problems*. The two men were plunging down a tar-black pit. To slow their fall, Hercules shot out a hand.

The wall was smooth and wet, too slick to grab. It sloped away from his fingers. The pit was growing wider. Hercules looked down again; he saw nothing but blackness.

He hit bottom so hard that he felt the ground vibrate. Instantly, Salmoneus crashed onto him, crushing Hercules' chest into the rough, rocky surface.

A stone door clapped shut behind and above them. Hercules could hear the clunk, slip and chop of a lead bar sliding into place, locking the door from the outside. *Fooled,* he thought bitterly. *Fooled and trapped.*

Salmoneus seemed to have six knees and eleven elbows, all poking into delicate parts of Hercules' body. Lying face up, Hercules tried to extract Salmoneus while Salmoneus tried to extract himself, leaving the two men more tangled than before. Somehow they managed to jam eight of Salmoneus' toes into Hercules' mouth.

"Weh wur wee wow wuh wy wow," Hercules said, as clearly as he could.

Salmoneus wiggled his toes until they popped out. "What?" he asked.

Hercules wiped his mouth with the back of his hand and spat. "I said, 'Get your feet out of my mouth,' " he said, scowling. He swallowed, and immediately was sorry that he had. "Don't you ever wash your feet?"

"Sure," said Salmoneus. "Just last month."

Hercules tried not to imagine what he had just swallowed. He stood, brushed off the dirt and rock fragments that covered his body, and looked around.

He could have seen more if he had closed his eyes. The pit was darker than midnight.

The guys who suckered me down here—how'd they get here without falling like we did? Hercules asked himself.

Maybe a rope ladder punched into the grass up top, he concluded. *Probably yanked it out of the ground when they got down here and pulled it after them. But where are they now?*

He stepped forward, walking carefully so as not to hurt himself on the craggy floor. He reached out until his fingers touched the wall, which was covered with the same slippery fluid as above.

His fingers slid along the wall, tracing the curved surface. They hit a thin gap. Hercules traced the gap with his fingernails: it was high, taller than he was, and it turned a corner, then another, and back down to the floor.

A door, he realized. He reached out to grab the handle, but it had none.

The door was a flat, wet, perfectly vertical slab, covered with a slick oil that made Hercules' fingers slip like a pig trying to ice-skate. Beneath the oil, his fingers felt only a cool sheet of metal that was polished to a flawless smoothness. Apparently, the rulers of this place had coated the door and walls with iron or another hard metal.

In Sparta, Hercules had seen craftsmen heat iron, lead, or even gold until it turned liquid, then pour the liquid metal onto a polished stone slab held up by ropes. When it cooled, the liquid turned solid and gave the stone a thick covering: layer upon smooth layer of practically unbreakable metal. Then the craftsmen painted some slippery oil on the door to prevent anyone from gripping it.

All right, Hercules thought, *so I can't grab it. There are other ways to open a door.*

He pulled his hand away. A thin film of the greasy goo stuck to his fingertips, and spiderweb-thin threads of the goo hung between his fingers like tiny hammocks. Ignoring the fluid, Hercules closed his hand into a fist, reared back on one leg, and hurled his body into a single punch.

His fist slipped on the slick door and slid across the surface. Though his knuckles screamed in pain, Hercules examined the effect of his punch.

The door's surface curved inward by only the thickness of a feather. He frowned at it. *Guess you need a little more.* He backed up several steps, dashed forward and rammed his shoulder into the door.

It bent in slightly where he had hit it but did not crack, leaving a round hollow as shallow as a saucer. His shoulder ached.

Better try something less painful, he thought. He slid his hands across the doorway until he found the thin gap between the wall and the door. He tried to lodge his fingers in the gap, but they were too thick.

He stuck his fingers out flat, a thin wedge projecting straight out from his wrist. He leaned back and shoved his fingertips into the gap, much as he'd shoved his fingers into the checkerboard square aboveground.

The door and wall were made of tougher stuff than the soft soil of the lawn. Hercules' fingers bounced back, covered in slippery grease. The impact jammed his fingernails back toward his knuckles. He grabbed his fingers with his other hand, gritted his teeth, and squinted his eyes shut, waiting for the pain to subside.

"Hercules?" Salmoneus asked.

This is not the time, Salmoneus, Hercules thought. He opened his eyes and groped the door in the dark, feeling for the damage that he'd done. His fingertips slid along the crack between door and wall; he found only a few fingernail-shaped nicks.

"But Herc," Salmoneus insisted, "it's important."

Hercules sighed. Turning in the direction of his friend's voice, he asked, "What is it?"

"Come here. I've found something."

Hercules shuffled cautiously along the rough floor. His foot thumped into something big and meaty, like a side of beef.

"That's it," Salmoneus said. "Just a second."

Hercules heard something scrape along the ground, and then a low hiss. The pit flared into view; Salmoneus was sitting on the ground, holding a wooden stick. Its wide top was burning.

"I got it from him," he said, pointing at the object at Hercules' feet. "Strike it along the ground, and it flames. I've got to sell something like this when we get to safety. I've got the product; now, I just need a name to match."

"Never mind that," Hercules said. He knelt and looked at the thing that had stopped him. It was covered in a lion skin that hid details of its appearance. The thing was lumpy and big, nearly seven feet long. It was narrow at one end, widening almost all the way to the other end, then it suddenly stopped, like a long, narrow pyramid. Something roughly round lolled atop the wide end.

Hercules pulled off the lion skin. Salmoneus bent over the object and stared at it. It was a man lying on his back, out cold.

The man on the ground was tall, broad-shouldered,

tanned, and handsome. His nose was straight; his chin was firm as mahogany; his skin was unblemished. His hair was shoulder-length and brown. His arms and chest were weighted down with muscle, and his legs looked strong as well. His eyes were closed.

"Hercules," Salmoneus said, "it's you."

Bringing the torch closer to the man, Salmoneus looked at him in brighter light. "Whoops, sorry, Herc. This guy looks kinda like you—but not really."

Hercules swept his gaze along the mystery man's body from foot to neck. He could see how someone could mistake the two for each other—they were roughly the same size, shape, and color—but Hercules found himself picking out the most obvious differences.

He's taller than me, Hercules thought. *Thicker in the legs than I am, slimmer in the waist, broader in the chest. More hair on the chest than I've got, too. He's got bigger hands and feet. Not to mention his arms—they look like oak trunks with muscles.*

The giant's skin, Hercules noticed, was rougher than his own. It was also a shade darker, as was his hair. His nose was longer and wider than Hercules', and the eyes were further apart. The eyebrows were thicker. His mouth was smaller, his lips thinner. His head was not as long as Hercules', and was flatter on top. A large, red bruise was on his forehead.

The stranger was breathing shallowly and slowly. Hercules knelt down and touched the man's face. The man stayed completely still.

He turned the man over. The giant's skin looked as bruised as Hercules' felt. Someone must have hurled the stranger into this pit, and he'd landed hard, back first, on the rocky floor. Hercules brushed dirt and pebbles off his back.

Hercules took one of the man's hands. *No rings, no bracelets*, he thought. *Nothing to identify him.* He let go of the hand.

"No one who's ever met you would mistake you for him," Salmoneus said. Realizing that he himself had done that very thing, he quickly added, "Well, at least not for long."

With a grunt of effort, Hercules turned the man over. Salmoneus pulled back the man's eyelid and looked up at Hercules. "His eyes are darker than yours, Herc," he said.

A hand grabbed his throat. The man on the ground bolted to his feet, clasping Salmoneus by the neck and dangling him above the ground. "What are you doing?" the man roared.

Salmoneus dropped the torch. It clattered onto the ground but stayed lit. He gurgled and kicked, but his feet hit nothing.

Hercules stepped forward. He looked up and stared the giant in the eyes. *This guy really is enormous,* he realized. *Still, I don't think he's a demigod. I could beat him in a fair fight*—Hercules' back and shoulders ached, and the wound in his leg throbbed painfully—*I think.*

"Put the man down," Hercules commanded, his voice cold, flat, and firm. "We saw you lying there. You were out cold. You might have been dying. We were examining you." He stared up into the man's eyes.

The man stared down hard at him, not blinking. His empty hand formed a fist. "Put the man down," Hercules repeated slowly.

"Or at least," Salmoneus gasped, his voice a strangled rasp, "let the man breathe." He clawed at the fingers around his neck but could not budge them.

Salmoneus won't last long this way, Hercules thought. Salmoneus tried to scream; no sound came out. *But if I even try to grab that ox's arm, he'll squeeze Salmoneus' neck like a blob of clay.* He imagined Salmoneus' skin oozing like mud between the man's fingers, the bones of Salmoneus' neck cracking like dry leaves under a heavy boot.

I need a plan. A strategy, and fast. Salmoneus was turning blue; his flailing grew weaker. Hercules scanned his opponent's face, looking for weaknesses. *Some tactic, something unpredictable.* His eyes slid down the giant's chest. *Something subtle and clever.* His gaze kept moving down. Salmoneus' eyes closed; his head flopped backward. His arms and legs hung limp.

The heck with cleverness. Hercules punched the giant in the belly.

The giant's fist sprang open, dropping Salmoneus. He bent double, grabbing his midsection with both hands and gasping. Salmoneus hit the floor like a rag doll.

The impact popped his eyes open. Salmoneus gulped air and panted, his body rising with each ravenous breath. *Thank Zeus you're all right,* Hercules thought.

He turned to the still-wheezing giant. "I don't want

to hit you again," he said. "Don't make me do it."

The giant stared down at him, curious. "You're . . . you're not one of *them*." His voice was deeper than Hercules', and he spoke slowly. He reminded Hercules of a black bear—big, strong, lumbering, deadly if provoked.

"No," Hercules said, settling onto the ground. He sat, cross-legged; Salmoneus did the same, placing himself safely behind his friend. As Salmoneus picked up his torch, Hercules patted the ground. "Sit. Let's talk."

The giant stood, his eyes wary. After a long moment, he said, "Yeah. All right," and lowered himself to the pit's floor. He landed heavily, with a low grunt.

"Takes the guy a while to make a decision, huh?" Salmoneus said quietly to Hercules. "Kinda like an eight-horse chariot pulled by two horses. It gets there, but it's not real swift."

"Quiet," Hercules muttered out of the corner of his mouth. He extended a hand for the giant to shake. "My name is Hercules," he said with a warm smile. "What's yours?"

The man rested his chin on his fist and gazed downward at nothing in particular. He looked to Hercules like a thoughtful four-year-old—a gargantuan, thoughtful four-year-old.

Another long silence; it seemed to Hercules that the giant was gauging whether his name was a piece of information harmless enough to give away.

"Cactus," the man said. He looked at Hercules and Salmoneus, watching for their reaction.

Hercules decided to give him one. "Interesting name," he said. "It's a plant, isn't it?"

The giant let out a long sigh; his entire body sagged and relaxed. He seemed relieved that Hercules hadn't made fun of his name. He must have been teased and insulted about it since shortly after birth.

"Yeah," he answered. "My mother gave it to me." He blushed and looked away. "It means 'Tough on the outside, sweet on the inside,' " he said softly.

He turned back to Hercules and looked him straight in the eye, his jaw tight with tension. "I'm telling that now 'cause it always comes out. I like to get it over with." His eyes seemed to search for something. "No jokes, okay?"

Hercules tried not to smile. He found himself liking the big, sensitive lunk. "You've got a deal," he said. He leaned back, trying to appear casual. He stopped when he felt his back brushing against Salmoneus. "So tell us, how'd you get down here?"

Another slow, long moment while Cactus studied Hercules' and Salmoneus' faces in the torchlight. Hercules tried to keep his face blank or at most blandly curious; Salmoneus stayed silent and tried not to show fear of the man who nearly throttled him.

Having finished his inspection, Cactus looked down, deep in thought. Salmoneus found himself itching in his armpits; he wondered if it would annoy the giant if he were to scratch. Finally, Cactus looked up and aimed his gaze at the men.

"I was being Hercules."

10

"How's that again?" Salmoneus asked. He couldn't help himself.

"I get it," Hercules said. "You're a—well, a Hercules impersonator."

Cactus nodded. "Don't make fun, okay? I'm not proud of it."

He looked Hercules up and down. "But *you* know what it's like. Not a lot of jobs out there for a guy who's—who's not real smart. I mean, maybe you're smart, but—oh, you know what I mean."

"I think so," said Hercules. "Go on, please."

"Yeah. Well, when you're big like me, people think you're Hercules. Even if you say you're not."

The giant stopped. He stayed silent for so long that Hercules thought he was finished. Several times, Cactus drew in a breath to speak and then decided against it.

Finally, in the guilty, reluctant tone of a little boy confessing that he broke his mother's favorite vase, he went on: "So one day, just for fun—well, just for fun and to get them off your back—you say, 'Yeah, I am Hercules.' And you know what they do." He waited for Hercules to answer.

"Sorry, I don't," Hercules said. "Can you tell me?"

Cactus reached forward and grabbed Hercules' shoulders, one in each massive hand. "But you know!" he insisted, shaking Hercules. "You do it, too, just like me. You know how it is."

Hercules gently removed Cactus' hands. "I'm sorry. I'm not a Hercules impersonator."

Cactus pulled away from Hercules. The giant leaned back and peered at him as if Hercules had just claimed to be the son of a god or something equally ridiculous. "But you said your name was Hercules. I figured you were just saying that 'cause you're like me. I thought you knew what it was like."

Cactus stared at the ground, clearly disappointed. *He'll never believe I'm not an impersonator*, Hercules thought.

"Well, *I* don't know what it's like," Salmoneus said. He sounded annoyed. "Tell me."

Cactus glanced over Hercules' shoulder and watched Salmoneus for a moment. The peddler shuddered; he began to doubt the wisdom of calling the thick-fingered giant's attention to him.

"All right," Cactus said. "Well, when people think you're Hercules, they're so glad to see you— you're a famous hero, you know—they give you

90

things. Food and ale and—girls." He looked down again and blushed.

He raised his head and took a deep breath. "Anyway, I went around from town to town, and I always got things. But after a while in a town, I always got sick of myself. Telling a lie about who I was and taking all that stuff."

Cactus leaned forward until he was no longer sitting but was riding on his knees. His muscles were as tight as harp strings. "And some of those towns were so poor! They were starving to give me steaks and fancy desserts, and I *tried* to tell 'em not to give me things, but they wouldn't listen. I guess they thought I could get Zeus to help 'em or something."

He sat down again, rocking back and forth a few times to calm himself. "So I always promised myself: in the next town, I won't say I'm Hercules. But the road between towns was always so long." Cactus stared off into nothingness, remembering. "I got tired and hungry and thirsty. And so lonely."

His gaze returned to Hercules. "Well, so I get to the next town. They start asking if I'm Hercules and putting juicy meats and sweet wines and pretty girls next to me and offering me soft pillows to sleep on. Then the children gather around. They want rides on my shoulders. And I give them rides, all the rides they want. Then—you should see it."

He smiled sadly. "They run away so happy. They're yelling all over town, 'I got to ride on Hercules! I got to ride on Hercules!' " The giant closed his eyes. "How could I tell 'em what I really am?"

Another long silence descended, blanketing the

room like a fog. This time, Cactus seemed truly finished speaking rather than simply deciding what (if anything) he would say next. Hercules filled the gap. "So you kept doing it, going from town to town as— as Hercules. How did you get into this dungeon?"

Cactus opened his eyes. "It started a couple weeks ago. Maybe three weeks. I was on the mainland. I—I freeloaded from Salonika all the way down to Athens." He paused. "I hated myself."

Another pause. "So I tried to get away from people, from presents, from—everything. I found a boat going from Athens to this island. The captain said there were people here, but if I wanted to be alone, I could hide in the forest.

"He let me ride on his boat for free. He said, 'Son, I can't charge you. Now that I've got the son of Zeus on board, we're sure to get smooth sailing and safe landing.' "

Another pause. Salmoneus couldn't stand it. "So what happened?" he shrilled.

Cactus looked at him with dead eyes. "The boat crashed on a reef. I'm the only one who made it to land alive."

"Oh," Salmoneus said. "Sorry."

"Thanks." Cactus took a deep breath. It seemed to Hercules that the story was getting more painful for the giant to tell. "So I wandered from the shore into a forest. I suppose it was about two nights ago. I heard someone giggling. A girl. She was hiding behind a tree."

* * *

The girl was slim but curvy, dressed in a filmy dress that showed off her long, slender legs. Her sleeveless blouse clung to her chest, exposed her tanned arms and shoulders to the flattering moonlight, and split into a hundred wispy fringes that didn't quite cover her belly and navel.

The tree in front of her was too thin to hide her, but then, she didn't want it to, any more than she wanted the dress to hide her soft, flat midriff. She batted her eyelashes at the muscular stranger, drawing his attention to her pale green eyes. She ran her fingers through her cascade of auburn hair, primping for the man's attention.

She giggled again. He stared at her, apparently amazed at his luck at finding such an enticing sight in the middle of the woods.

I bet she thinks I'm Hercules, he thought. *What do I do?* She wiggled her fingers at the stranger in a charming little wave and spun like a dancer.

Suddenly, she was gone, dashing on tiptoe into the forest. *This is the last time I say I'm him,* he thought. *I promise.* He shot after her.

The girl was bounding through the woods fast enough to stay out of the man's hands but slowly enough to stay in his sight. The giant crashed through bushes and trees, determined to catch her.

"Come here, girl!" he shouted. "Please come here. Don't you know me? I'm Hercules!"

She said nothing but just giggled again.

The girl ducked behind a rock taller than she was. The giant sped up and veered behind the rock.

The girl was gone. She must have changed course

and bolted behind a tree while out of his sight.

He heard someone tiptoeing behind him. "Oh, Hercules," a musical voice called. With a happy smile, he turned.

A different woman was facing him, older than the girl, but with blond hair, blazing blue eyes, and flawless, snowy skin. She had her arms raised high above her head and began to swing them down.

"And that's all I remember. She hit me with a club, I guess," Cactus finished. "When I woke up, I was here. I had a headache—" he touched the bump on his forehead—"and a whole lot of bruises. I hit the ground hard, I guess."

Makes sense, Hercules thought. *Slaughterius must be using Dryope and her dryad girls to patrol the forest near his city. Maybe that's why he hooked up with her.*

Hercules chewed a knuckle as another thought came to him. "Cactus, have you ever been to Mercantilius?"

Cactus looked at him, his expression blank as a new sheet of paper. "To where?"

"Never mind." Hercules got up; he needed to stretch and refresh his body and brain.

He's a likable guy, he thought. *He tells a great story. But is it true? I've never heard of Dryope clubbing someone. Of course, that doesn't mean that she couldn't.*

"Hercules," Salmoneus said.

"Not now, Salmoneus," Hercules muttered. *What if Cactus is the impostor who killed the Mercantili-*

ans? He's passed for me before, he says. And he did try to kill Salmoneus.

No, wait a second. Cactus doesn't look enough like me to fool anyone who's seen me—and the Mercantilians have seen me. Cactus can't be the impostor.

Still, maybe he found a way to change his looks. Maybe he's not really dumb but only playing dumb. Maybe he's—

"Herc!" Salmoneus called, tugging at his friend's shirt.

Hercules turned. "All right, Salmoneus. What is it?"

Salmoneus pointed upward. "We've got guests," he said. "I think they've been watching for a while."

Hercules tilted his head back and looked up through a long stretch of blackness. The blackness framed a square of night sky, with clouds drifting out of the square to uncover a filmy, white spray of bright stars.

Something dark blocked a corner of the square. It had an irregular shape, all round bumps. Hercules felt as though he should recognize it.

"Hello, clown," the black shape crooned in a familiar, fluty voice. He slapped his cheek with a languid hand. "Oh, I am so *rude*! That's the wrong way to greet an old friend." The voice changed, growing deeper, dropping its odd lisp. "I meant, 'Hello, Hercules.' "

11

Slaughterius, Hercules thought. *He fooled me. Put on that fake voice to make me think he was a weak-brained idiot. And I fell for it!*

"You're a very poor faker, you know," Slaughterius said. "We saw through that clown disguise right away."

Another, curvier shape joined Slaughterius' silhouette. Dryope linked an arm with the Pastoralian. Hercules could not see her smug, tight-lipped smile.

He didn't have to; he could hear it in her voice. "Did you really think I wouldn't remember you," she asked, her tone slipping into steely anger, "after the way you *rejected* me last month?"

"That's the voice," Cactus whispered. "That's the woman who hit me!"

The dryad queen calmed herself. She went on, "I knew it was you right away."

"Hold it," Hercules said. "I haven't seen you since that big party on Olympus."

Hercules remembered the occasion well. It took place years earlier, on the anniversary of Zeus' dethroning Kronos, the king of the gods before Zeus. He had summoned all of the gods and demigods to a festival celebrating the occasion.

The party had quickly grown rowdy, as celebrations among the gods often did. Ares kept grabbing Hercules by the butt, throwing him to the ground, and demanding that he wrestle. Hermes and Apollo forced Hercules to choose which of the two was the better musician; when Hercules chose Apollo, Hermes tried to pull Hercules' ears off. Pan, drunk, cornered Hercules and complained—endlessly—that he himself, not Zeus, defeated Kronos, because he sang his own creation, the fear called panic, into Kronos' ears and terrified him into fleeing.

And Dryope had tried to lure Hercules into her arms. Lovely though the queen of the forest nymphs had been, Hercules had seen that she had wanted him only for his muscular body, to use and discard as if he had been a cake of soap.

But that had been long ago. "I didn't reject you last month," Hercules said. "I didn't even see you last month."

Dryope and Slaughterius laughed. "Very funny," the general said. "Next, you'll say that the earth isn't flat, or some even more outlandish lie."

"Slaughterius," Hercules called urgently, "please listen. You can do what you want to us, but you have to understand: the Mercantilians are going to attack your city in the morning. Ares is spreading lies to inflame them to war.

"But—listen to me!—you can stop it. You can kill the lies if you'll just work *with* the Mercantilians. I know they don't trust you, so you'll have to send them an ambassador, somebody neutral, maybe someone from another city-state. Have them contact the Mercantilians." Hercules' neck began to hurt from the strain of bending backward and yelling upward, but he kept talking. "If you can just talk honestly to each other, you can—"

Slaughterius and Dryope were laughing again. "Thank you for giving away my enemies' secret strategy, Hercules," Slaughterius sang out. "Now, do excuse me. I simply must get ready to wipe them out."

"So long, lover boy," Dryope added. "So sad you didn't take your chance with me while you could." The two black shapes receded from the grassy edge of the starry-skyed square.

Hercules bent deep at the knees and sprang skyward. *Got to grab that square while it's still open!*

He was rising faster than Helios and his chariot, the night air hissing in his ears and whisking his face. He looked up and saw the starry, hard-edged hole grow closer and the stars grow larger. *I'm gonna make it.*

The air grew quieter in his ears. His rise began to slow down. He looked up again. Stretching his arms and fingers forward, the world's strongest man reached for the edge of the grass square.

It lay too far above him to touch.

He began to fall. The air rushed in his ears as he plunged into the darkness. Hercules reached out for the wall of the pit, but his fingers slid off, just as they had during his first descent.

His ribs still ached from the first time he had hit the pit's rocky bottom. He looked down and knew it was rushing up to meet him.

This, he thought, *is going to hurt.*

It did. Greatly. The ground shimmied under the impact, and the rocks cut into his back again. Cactus and Salmoneus each took an arm and helped Hercules to his feet.

Something rumbled up above. "Not bad, Hercules," came Slaughterius' voice. "You must have cleared eight levels. But don't bother trying again. I've got a little gift for you. I was saving it for the Mercantilians tomorrow, but it's all yours tonight."

Hercules looked up. *He was saving it?* Hercules thought. *He knew about the war all along!*

He saw a round, black shape inch into the square hole. Metal squeaked against metal as the shape turned. Something gurgled and sizzled.

A stream of thick, red fluid dropped down. The shape, Hercules realized, was a cauldron.

"Back up!" Hercules called. "Get against the walls!" At top speed, all three men backpedaled. Hercules felt the wall's cool oil and cold metal slap his skin.

The fluid hit the center of the rocky floor with a splash. Cactus and Salmoneus screamed.

Hercules knew why. The droplets bounced up from the floor and splashed onto his thigh, stinging his skin as if it had been burned. He looked down and saw a blotchy, bloody hole there, steaming.

The liquid was acid.

In the starlight, Hercules saw red liquid eating bloody trails in his flesh, while it merely slid off the glistening walls.

The acid was puddling in the middle of the floor, steaming and bubbling. As more and more flowed from the walls onto the floor, the red liquid spread, reaching toward his friends' feet—and his own.

That stuff's not going to eat an escape hatch through the walls, he thought. *It's not going to burn a hole through the floor. It's just going to eat us.*

As the acid continued to pour from the sky, rivers of red oozed from the middle of the floor toward every edge and corner. A quick downhill stream headed for Salmoneus' feet. He shifted away, but the acid slid through the fissures between the floor's rocks, splitting into a dozen rivulets that chased him wherever he went. He stood on tiptoe, his back arched toward the wall and away from the oncoming liquid.

The river hit his toes. Salmoneus shrieked. He dropped the torch; it fizzled in the acid and went out, leaving the room lit only by thin starlight from above. The shrieking continued in the near blackness.

Hercules could hear the acid sizzling and smell his friend's skin melting. *I can't stand this,* he thought.

He slid around the waterfall of acid and dived toward Salmoneus' feet. Bending low, Hercules ripped acid-covered rocks from the floor.

The acid fell away from Salmoneus and into the small crater that Hercules was digging. The liquid touched his fingers, and he yanked them away. He felt as if someone was razoring his skin open.

Cactus screamed. He was trying to be brave, but the acid had slid over his toes and heels and was pooling over the top of his feet. Smoke rose from the rising pond of redness.

Hercules edged along the walls and knelt at Cactus' feet. As the acid slid over the floor, he could feel it biting his knees like a hundred sharp-toothed cats. He ripped rocks from the floor, cutting out a deep valley, and the crimson tide slipped from Cactus' feet toward Hercules' digging hands.

I can't keep this up forever, he thought, wincing against the liquid's hot stabs. With both hands, he grabbed the edge of a huge, square rock poking out of the ground and yanked, hoping to pull it out and leave a wide hole where the acid would collect.

The top edge of the rock broke off in his hands.

In frustration, he pounded the floor. Splinters of rock flew, and the floor vibrated slightly, just as it had when he had fallen on it.

Hercules' mouth fell open. *It shouldn't do that. If that's solid ground, it shouldn't move.*

Unless it's not the ground. . . .

Hercules clasped his hands tight and swung them into the pit's floor. He felt rock shatter; jagged chunks floated to the surface of the shallow acid lake that now covered the floor and kept rising as more acid fell from above. The acid dissolved his sandals and started eating into his feet, but Hercules continued to pound the floor. He felt as if the acid were ripping his skin off.

He fell forward into the acid, his arms dropping into it all the way to the elbow.

"Hercules!" Salmoneus screamed, temporarily forgetting his own burning agony. He saw something even more frightening than Hercules' collapse into the flesh-eating liquid.

As Hercules pulled out his arms, he was smiling. "Oh, dear lord," Salmoneus said, "he's gone nuts."

As the acid dribbled down his forearms, cutting channels as it went, Hercules dug a canal to Salmoneus' feet.

The acid pooling toward Salmoneus turned away. It slid into the new canal and drained toward the spot where Hercules had fallen. Hercules cut another channel from Cactus' feet, and the acid slipped from him as well.

The flow from above was slowing. It became a trickle, then a few drops, then nothing. Hercules looked up; the cauldron was empty and rolling away.

Salmoneus stared at the floor. There was a hole in it the size of Hercules' fist. The last drips of acid slid along the channels that he had dug, and slipped down the hole, hissing

Through the hole, Hercules could see another pit, possibly as deep as the one that held himself, Cactus, and Salmoneus.

Hercules heard a creak from above. He looked up and saw a black shape closing over the hole to the surface world. The black shape's borders told Hercules what it was: the checkerboard square of lawn that served as the hole's lid. *So long, escape route,* he thought.

With a dull thump, the square covered the hole. It cut off the last of the starlight, blanketing the pit in darkness.

Someone moaned. "Salmoneus," Hercules asked, "was that you?"

"I'm too wiped out to groan," the peddler said.

"Wasn't me, either," Cactus offered.

The groan sounded again. It was coming from the hole in the floor. "Stand back, guys," Hercules said. He slid his fingertips along the floor, searching for the hole. A thin film of acid coated the floor's stony surface; Hercules jerked back his hand. *Steady*, he told himself; *just find the hole*.

He kept trying. His fingers hit empty air, and he nearly fell face first as his arm dropped into the hole.

The hole in the floor beneath Hercules ran as deep as his forearm. He lay down on the rocks, trying to ignore the hot, red juice devouring the skin of his belly and chest.

Hercules wrapped his fingers around the bottom of the hole and gripped the floor's underside. The surface was dry of both acid and slick oil; a wave of relief washed over him. "Here it comes, guys," he said.

With a two-handed yank, the world's strongest man tore a thick chunk of floor out from under himself. The floor cracked; a jagged line ran to the wall where Cactus stood.

He heard Cactus suck in a gasp. "You really are him," he said softly. He sounded as if he were praying. "You're Hercules."

"You betcha," Salmoneus replied.

Again Hercules grabbed rock, ripping out chunk after chunk until the hole was wide enough for a man. He heard someone below groan once more, only fainter; whoever was getting hurt sounded close to death.

"I'm going down, guys," Hercules said.

"Uh, Herc?" Salmoneus asked. "You mind if we don't go with you? See, the pain from that acid is still really sharp, and the acid spilled down there, and we—"

"I understand," Hercules replied. "You rest. I'll be back." He grabbed the edge of the hole and lowered himself carefully.

As he passed below the pit's floor, he could see a dim, flickering light illuminating the walls. The area below was a hallway.

Hercules could smell the bitter aroma of the acid pools on the hallway's ground. *If I drop down, I'll hit acid*, he thought. His skin was tender and sore from sinking into acid; he did not want that experience again.

Hanging by his fingertips, Hercules began to swing back and forth. With each swing, he pushed himself further and higher, until his toes flew nearly to the ceiling.

Another swing. His fingers let go, and he went flying.

He landed just clear of the acid pools. As he skidded to a halt on his knees, the rocks of the underground floor tore red lines in his skin.

For a moment, Hercules simply sat on a mercifully dry rock. *Lord, my skin hurts*, he thought.

He looked around. The dark rock walls of the hall-way were lined with torches. Resting in metal half-cones, they flickered brightly and made shadows that wavered and danced.

From around a curve up ahead, Hercules heard a familiar groan, followed by the unmistakable thump of fist against flesh. A whimper arose, but a sharp slap cut it off.

Hercules gritted his teeth, hungry to get his hands on whoever was hurting the victim around the corner—but he stopped himself. *Could be another trap*, he thought. With agonizing slowness, he inched forward and turned the corner.

The hallway stretched before him. At the far end, its walls curved toward each other until they almost touched. Light poured through the gap between the walls.

Hercules backed up against one of the walls and sidled toward the light. When he reached the wall's curved end, he peeked through the gap.

He saw a wide chamber, its walls and ceiling coated in the same slick metal as the pit. The chamber was roughly round, but its walls wove in and out, forming deep nooks and alcoves. In the middle of the room, at least fifty feet in front of Hercules, was a rectangular stack of hot rocks, coloring the walls with a hellish glow.

Behind the rocks stood a Pastoralian soldier, bulk-ier than Hercules. He wore a chain mail shirt and was heavily armed. A club hung from each hip, and a bow and quiver of arrows were strapped to his back.

Although the soldier was facing Hercules, he didn't

seem to notice him. The soldier was concentrating on an old man, whom he had clutched by the back of the neck, and was making kneel over the rocks.

The old man was painfully thin; his skin sagged from his bones like wet clothes on a line. He wore a dirty bunch of scraps and tatters that had once been a sleek, tailored toga. A fat drop of sweat rolled down the old man's grimy forehead and nose, and fell onto the rocks; it immediately sizzled, bubbled, and vanished, leaving only a wisp of steam.

The old man looked roughly familiar to Hercules, but he had no time to puzzle over his identity. *I can't let that guy get tortured*, Hercules thought. *Trap or no trap, here I come!*

The old man looked up. Apparently, he had sensed or expected his arrival. Seeing Hercules about to spring, the old man started to mouth the word *no*.

The soldier licked his lips, opened them in a gap-toothed sneer, and pushed the old man's face toward the roasting rocks. Their light colored his skin red.

Hercules sprinted toward the soldier.

The old man grabbed a red-hot rock in each hand and, ignoring the pain of his own searing palms, thrust the rocks into the soldier's face.

The soldier screamed, clutching at his scorched cheeks. As he wheeled about, blind with pain, Hercules saw the old man drop the rocks and run toward a nook in the wall. Hercules shifted course and followed him.

A club flew past Hercules' shoulder and landed on the ground nearby. The top of the club was a circle of spikes and grooves, like a king's crown, each spike as long as a man's hand and sharper than an adder's fang. It had come from a nook in the wall: the old man's destination.

Hercules realized that if he had kept going foward and not turned to follow the old man, the club would have struck him dead center in the chest and punctured a lung. *That man saved my life!*

The old man disappeared into the shadowy nook from which the club had flown. Hercules chased after him.

Before Hercules could enter the darkness, a soldier tumbled out of the nook with a club dangling from a hip holster, and the old man clamped around his legs. Squeezing the soldier's knees together and pulling them forward, the old man was yanking him to the ground.

The two men landed at Hercules' feet. Hercules grabbed the soldier's shoulders and pulled him up.

The old man, dangling from the soldier's knees, looked alarmed at something behind Hercules. Dropping to the rock floor of the cavern, the old man ran back toward the pile of hot rocks.

Hercules turned to see the old man sprinting toward the soldier who had tried to push his face into the rocks. Recovering from his burns, the soldier was trying to aim a bow and arrow at Hercules' chest. The soldier waved the arrow left, right, up, and down, but the onrushing old man, waving his arms, blocked him from getting a clear shot.

Still holding the other soldier in midair, Hercules saw the archer's bow stop bobbing and take a steady bead on the old man's chest. The other soldier, seeing

Hercules distracted, grabbed his club and swung it at Hercules' gut.

It never touched him. Hercules, ignoring the club, flung the soldier into the air. Sailing in a graceful arc that almost grazed the cavern's ceiling, he whistled over the old man's head and crashed into the bowman, sending him stumbling backward onto the hard, rocky ground.

The bowman got to his feet, only to find Hercules leaping onto him. Hercules pulled the bowman to his feet, grabbing the other soldier as he rose. He lifted both men, cracked their heads together, and dropped them by the hot rocks. They looked surprisingly peaceful, napping in the rocks' sunset-red glow.

Hercules turned to face the old man. He was sitting on the ground near the middle of the cavern, between the shadowy nook and the hot rocks. He trembled and wheezed, but his head was tilted up, his eyes attentive.

As Hercules approached him, the old man jerked his head to the right. Hercules glanced in that direction.

In the smooth, wet wall, polished like the others to a mirrored finish, he saw the reflection of three soldiers in a nook on the opposite wall. One of them was aiming a bow and arrow, with a heavy, jagged head, at his ribs. The others aimed slightly behind and in front of him; if he tried to escape by moving forward or backward, they would shoot him. Hercules could tell by the way they held their weapons that they were experts in targeting and killing.

He suddenly felt very tired of people aiming deadly objects at him.

Hercules' hands were empty. He stood in the middle of a mostly empty floor; he had no weapons to stop the men and no way to reach any weapons.

Or did he? He looked down. *This is going to hurt—but not as much as getting skewered by an arrow.* He clasped his hands together and raised them over his head. With all the force in his god-spawned body, he swung his fists into the ground as an arrow whizzed over his head.

The rocky floor shook and splintered as if a bomb had hit it. Hundreds of shards flew into the air and clattered on the ground.

An arrow whizzed between Hercules' arm and his chest, slicing off several armpit hairs. Another shaft ripped some skin off of his ear.

Well, I'll be dipped in manure, Hercules thought, amazed. *I didn't even slow them down.* He grabbed an armful of shards and began running toward the archers, hurling the pieces toward them.

Two arrows immediately struck the shards out of his hands.

An arrow sank into the dagger wound in his thigh, ripping it open and sending blood gushing out. Hercules dropped to his knees in pain, near one of the unconscious guards. Too late, he realized that he had made himself a perfect target.

Then he realized that no more arrows were flying toward him.

Hercules looked up. Cactus was standing between

him and the archers. The giant must have entered only seconds before.

"Who are you?" one of the archers asked. "I warn you, we have to kill him. But we've got no quarrel with you."

Cactus did not speak. Hercules guessed at what was going through the giant's mind. *He can get away clean*, Hercules thought. *He doesn't even have to say anything. All he has to do is join their side and attack me. He's lied before, just to catch a girl or a meal. Now, it's his life.*

Finally, the giant spoke. "My name is Cactus. I am the friend of this man behind me."

The archers fired. "Cactus, duck!" Hercules shouted. As the giant hit the floor, the arrows flew over his head.

The archers took aim at Hercules.

Hercules ripped off the chain mail shirt of the guard on the floor and threw it in their faces. Momentarily confused by the heavy mesh, they dropped their bows to pull it off.

Cactus attacked. Hercules watched in awe. He had seen some efficient fighters, but few as swift and powerful as the giant. Within seconds, the archers were sleeping.

Hercules yanked the arrow from his leg, tore off a strip of his shirt, and wrapped it around his thigh as a bandage. He heard heavy footsteps crunching toward him, and felt the coolness of an enormous shadow, big enough for four men, slipping over him. He looked up.

"Where do you want these guys?" Cactus asked,

holding three unconscious archers in one hand. "I heard you having a fight, so I came down to help. Is that okay?"

"Okay?" Hercules grinned. "It's sensational. Thanks." He noticed fresh acid stains along Cactus' legs. "Are you all right?" he asked. "Did you fall into the acid pools?"

"Yeah," Cactus replied. He rubbed one of his wounds. He slumped to the ground and sat heavily, dumping the soldiers on the ground next to him. "Hurts pretty bad."

"Great work, Hercules!" shouted the cheery voice of Salmoneus. "I knew you could do it!"

Hercules turned to see his friend come around the edge of the chamber's entrance. Salmoneus, cheerful as a cat in a rat's nest, raised a triumphant fist and whirled it in wide loops through the sweaty air. "Ya-hoo!" he shouted. "What a fight! If you'd let me set you two up some gladiatorial battles, we'd make a bundle!"

Sweat dropped from Hercules' forehead into his eyes. He rubbed it away. "Salmoneus—where in Zeus' name were you? Maybe it didn't occur to you, but we could have used your help."

"That's what I was doing, pal," Salmoneus oozed.

The peddler bounced over to Hercules and tried to wrap a comradely arm around his shoulder. Since Hercules was far taller and wider than Salmoneus, he ended up with his palm on Hercules' neck. Hercules scowled; Salmoneus slid his arm off rapidly and wiped away the sweat that it had absorbed from Hercules' hot skin.

"You see," Salmoneus went on, "I was your secret reinforcement, like those three archers were the secret reinforcements for those two other hunks. If ever your enemies thought that they really had you, I'd spring out and—" he whipped into a fighting pose, all angles, with his hands flat and elbows bent. "Hah! Ho! Hoo!" Salmoneus chopped and kicked the air in what he believed was a fearsome display of violence.

"Sure," said Hercules. He didn't buy a word of Salmoneus' explanation, but he had more important situations to handle. He limped over to the old man sitting cross-legged on the floor.

As he approached, Hercules noted that the man would be quite tall if his shoulders weren't bent and he hadn't been shriveled by neglect and rough handling. The sides of his chest had thin, deep ridges where his ribs nearly poked through his flesh. Hercules wondered when the old man had eaten last.

The man's fingers were thin, as if even they were starving. Grime and soot covered his hands and the bottoms of his bare feet. His thin, nearly white hair was falling out; his beard was days old and scraggly. The pale skin of his cheeks sank into dark hollows below his tired, gray eyes.

Sudden coughs shook the man's body. Hercules half expected to hear the man's bones rattle. As when he first saw the man, Hercules found his face familiar.

"Pardon me," the man rasped. His voice was scratchy and faint, but deep as a bull's bellow. He cleared his throat, spat out some phlegm, and smiled weakly at Hercules. "Dungeon life does wonders for the old lungs," he joked.

"Hey, fella, you're a pretty tough fighter yourself!" Salmoneus called. He trotted over to the man's side. "Nobody expects an old guy to do what you did. I could sell you anywhere, from Africa to Siberia. You'd make the crowds go wild! And all three of you guys together, well . . ." He pulled the old man over to Hercules and Cactus. "One for four!" he shouted, "And three for—"

The old man laid a hand over Salmoneus' mouth. "Thanks," Hercules said.

The old man removed his hand, rubbed it on his toga, and raised a finger to his lips. He leaned close to Salmoneus.

"Don't shout," he said softly. "You might wake the sleeping beauties." He glanced at the unconscious soldiers. "What's worse, you might alert the guards outside."

The old man seemed perfectly comfortable giving orders to men much bigger and stronger than himself. Suddenly, Hercules realized why the man seemed familiar. It didn't make sense, it was an idiotic idea, it wasn't even possible. As he studied the man's face, though, he knew that he couldn't escape it.

"You're—" he began, but the old man knew what he was going to say.

"Yes, Hercules," the old man said. "I am Slaughterius."

12

Hercules felt very heavy, as if he were carrying buckets of bricks. *Okay*, he told himself, *this whole situation is completely confusing. And it comes on top of a whole pile of other things that are completely confusing.* He shook his head to clear it and took a deep breath to revive himself. *Best to just dive in and get used to it.*

"You need an explanation," the old man said, smiling gently. "Come, sit."

"Several explanations," Hercules agreed. He sat down next to the old man, and Salmoneus sat down next to Hercules. Cactus sat opposite the three. "If you're Slaughterius, who's the guy up there?" Hercules asked. He cocked a thumb at the ceiling.

"Frankly," the old man said, "that's what I would like to know." A spasm of coughing exploded through him. He took several wheezy breaths and went on.

Some weeks ago, he said, rumors began spreading that the cows and sheep raised by the citizens of Pastoralis were unfit for human use. Sales dropped like a rock pushed off a cliff.

Since the Pastoralians made their living from their trade in livestock, wool, beef, mutton, and other products of cows and sheep, they soon found themselves broke. They couldn't afford to buy anything from other cities, including food, clothing, or any comforts or luxuries. Pastoralians who could find work elsewhere soon did, leaving the town nearly empty of doctors, teachers, carpenters, and other skilled workers.

As leader of Pastoralis, Slaughterius promised to fix the situation. Whenever tourists or traders came to town (the few who still did), Slaughterius had his guards bring the visitors to him so that he could question them and find out the source of the rumors. Getting the source from the visitors was surprisingly easy. They were happy to reveal it.

"Let me guess," Hercules said. "It was Mercantilius."

"Quite right," Slaughterius said. "How did you know?"

"I've heard something like this before," Hercules said. "Go on with the story."

In any event, Slaughterius met with Ferocius, the leader of the Mercantilians. The meeting slid into arguments, accusations, and name-calling. Slaughterius, seeing that the two sides would only get angrier if they kept shouting in each other's faces, took his people home.

That night, a squad of Pastoralian guards was on patrol around the city when someone killed them with Mercantilian spears. In a rude little touch, the attackers stole the guards' custom-made clubs. Clearly, the Mercantilians had sent a squad of their own on a mission of murder.

"It was an act of war," Slaughterius said. "At dawn, I sent an entire platoon of our best soldiers, howling for revenge, over the long forest ridge that separates our city from theirs."

Slaughterius paused for a moment. His head dropped, and he gazed down in the general direction of the hot rocks, staring at nothing.

"I should have sent more men," he muttered. "I figured that the Mercantilians were just a bunch of shopkeepers, not strong outdoor types like us. Besides, they'd attacked our territory once; they might do it again, so I wanted to keep the bulk of my soldiers here to protect my people. Maybe if I'd sent more men out on the attack, they wouldn't have been—have been . . ."

Slaughterius buried his head between his fists. His body quaked with sobs. Hercules laid a hand on his shoulder.

"I know," Hercules said gently. "The Mercantilians told me. They said that they turned your troops back."

Slaughterius' head swiveled. To Hercules' surprise, the sadness had vanished, replaced by a sharp glare, a jaw as firm as granite, an onyx-hard face, and eyes dark and gleaming with anger.

"Did they tell you how many of my troops they killed?" Slaughterius demanded. "Did they tell you how their spears punched holes in those young bodies and sent lifeblood gushing out?" He paused to let the words drill into Hercules' mind. More calmly, he added, "Thank Zeus the commander knew when he was defeated and brought the boys home. Enough of them died as it was."

Slaughterius wiped his eyes and nose with one of the scraps of his clothing. His voice softened, sounding almost pleading. "We've always been so peaceful. Just shepherds and herdsmen, you know. Our neighbors were always our trading partners, not enemies." He scratched thoughtfully behind his ear. As if his fingernail were uncovering an long-buried idea, he went on, "Oh, generations ago, before we discovered the benefits of trade and peace, we had wars— my ancestors dug this network of caves for us to hide our children and other loved ones. I expanded the tunnels and moved many of my people into them when war looked likely.

"But I never really believed that I'd have to send boys to their deaths."

The old man ran a hand through his hair; a few strands drifted to the floor. "I visited all the soldiers' parents and sweethearts, and apologized. It took more than a week." He closed his eyes. "The worst part was explaining to children why their daddies died."

Slaughterius shook his head vigorously, as if to fling the memories away like a dog shaking off a bath.

He sucked in a deep breath and opened his eyes. He stood, his back straight, and eyes sharp. Hercules could believe that he was looking at the ruler of a city-state.

"Well," Slaughterius said, his voice firm and level, "clearly, we had to counterattack. But we had a few problems. We knew the Mercs could probably match us for troop strength. Plus we'd be fighting on their turf. So we would need some special advantage."

Slaughterius shook his head and smiled ruefully, as if recalling some secret bit of foolishness that seemed almost amusing. He looked down at Hercules, still smiling. "And then you came along."

"Me?" Hercules asked. "It wasn't me."

Slaughterius raised an eyebrow. "Oh? He claimed to be Hercules, and he certainly looked like you. Perhaps you have a twin brother?"

No, Hercules thought, *just a half brother named Ares*. "There's an impostor running around claiming to be me."

Slaughterius glanced at Cactus out of the corner of his eye. "Ah, of course. You two don't look much like each other, but there must be ways to—"

"Wait a minute," Hercules said, "He's not the impostor."

Slaughterius raised both eyebrows. "Truly? Well, we can go into that later," he said. "Back to my story.

"In planning that terrible first raid, I had done at least one thing right. I instructed two of our slyest boys to let themselves be taken prisoner in order to enter the Mercantilian camp and spy on it.

"They learned that a great hero was there: the mighty Hercules, the slayer of great beasts, the warrior unparalleled. We knew of him—you—whoever from travelers who told us about Hercules' nobility, his self-sacrifice, his willingness to fight for anyone with a true need and a just cause."

Hercules looked looked down and smiled, pleased but embarrassed. "Thank you. It's nice to hear, but travelers sometimes exaggerate."

"They certainly do," Slaughterius replied. Hercules' head snapped back up to see if Slaughterius was making fun of him. Slaughterius wore a fatherly expression, gentle and wise. As the leader of a city-state, he no doubt had suffered from untrue rumors himself.

"In any event," Slaughterius continued, "my spies contacted this 'Hercules.' The next day, just before dawn, when the town was asleep, you—I mean him, the fake Hercules—knocked out the jail guards and freed my men. They brought him to Pastoralis."

"I've heard this story," Hercules said. "At least some of it. What happened next?"

"Well," Slaughterius said. He paused, gathering his thoughts, and took in a long breath. " 'Hercules' was the most selfish, repulsive, fussy, insulting, bossy, unfair, pig-mannered, girl-clutching, ale-sucking excuse for a hero I had ever seen." Slaughterius' mouth curled into a scowl, and his nose wrinkled. "He had bad breath, too. Smelled like last night's cheese, which it probably was."

Hercules clapped a palm to his forehead. "Oh, brother," he moaned. "No wonder they tossed me down here."

"Well, no," Slaughterius said. "Not exactly. When I met you—him, I mean—and heard my spies' reports, I grew suspicious. Not just because of your—his—personal habits.

"You see, it struck me: Did I really want to trust the lives of my people to someone who would sell out the Mercantilians for a promise of sweetmeats and sweet wenches?" Slaughterius shook his head. "Of course not.

"He must have noticed my reluctance to get him involved in the war. He began bragging about how he'd led battles that had saved the towns of Itea and Levhadia and Navpatkos."

Slaughterius allowed himself a grim, tight-lipped smile. "Stupid of him. My people and I used to trade frequently with those towns—they're just across the Gulf of Corinth from us—and we knew that he had never rescued them from anything."

His smile faded. His face took on the hard coldness of raw stone as he counted on his fingers. "A glutton, a womanizer, a drunk, a traitor, and now a liar. I spent the rest of the afternoon alone, working out a plan to get rid of him.

"I worked through dinner and into the evening. He came to complain to me about some trival problem—his soup was cold, something like that—but I wouldn't see him."

Another tight-lipped smile. "Stupid of *me*. I should have behaved as I normally would with an honored guest: listened to him, fixed the problem, and gotten back to work. But I thought that figuring out how to ship an uncontrollable demigod far from my city was my top priority.''

He sighed sadly. "I'm not meant to be a military strategist. By neglecting him and holing up all alone, I only made him suspicious of me.''

"I see where this is going," Hercules said. "He attacked you and threw you down here.''

"More or less," Slaughterius agreed. He sat, rejoining Hercules and Salmoneus on the ground. "I was at work in my office, and heard footsteps behind me. I turned around—and the next thing I knew, I was in the dungeon.'' He rubbed the back of his neck and winced. "With quite a nasty bruise.''

"Then who's he?" Salmoneus asked, pointing upward. "You know, the fake version of you.''

"I have no idea," Slaughterius said. "An impostor, I suppose. I haven't seen him, just heard about him from the guards.'' He jerked a thumb at the unconscious soldiers lying on the cavern floor. "They came down here to rough me up, probably so I wouldn't look like—well, like me.''

"Then he—the fake you—can claim to be the only real Slaughterius," Hercules realized. "That's why that soldier was going to stick your face in the hot coals—to burn you beyond recognition.''

"Hey!" Salmoneus, who had been lounging, sat straight up. "Why didn't Slaughterius—the fake Slot, I mean—just kill you?''

It was a rude question. Silence hung in the air for a moment.

"You'd have to ask him," Slaughterius finally said. "Offhand, if I were in his sandals, I'd keep me around. After all, I know how Pastoralis works. If he runs into a problem and needs advice, he'll probably come down here to torture it out of me.

"And besides," he added, picking up a chip of rock and tossing it idly from hand to hand, "I do have my uses. I don't think it was any coincidence that the guards chose to torture me at the moment they did. They were using me to trap you." He scratched his belly with the chip. "Smart of them."

Slaughterius rubbed the back of his neck, still sore from the tight grip that the bowman had clamped on it. He looked at Hercules. "In any event, when you leaped to save me, I realized that the 'Hercules' I had met had been an impostor. He would never have saved me."

Slaughterius looked Hercules up and down. "Besides, those scars you've got"—he pointed at the gash on Hercules' leg and his other wounds—"are not something that 'my' Hercules, that sissy fraud, would have let himself get."

The old man leaned back and chewed a nail. His face looked thoughtful. "Now, I don't know if you're the real Hercules. You may be strong enough—you're certainly stronger than any man I've ever met—and you act like Hercules: you nearly gave your life for me. Still, of course, that doesn't prove that you're him, or any other kind of god."

He stood, and waved for Hercules to follow. "But Hercules or no Hercules," Slaughterius said, "you're a good man." He turned to Cactus, who had been silent the entire time, drinking the words in and weighing them carefully. "And so are you," Slaughterius said. He offered the men his hand to shake, presenting it between them.

Hercules accepted it, wrapping his huge palm and fingers around the smaller man's thinner ones. Cactus hesitated—he didn't seem to know where to put his own hand—then settled on laying it atop Hercules'.

Salmoneus sprang to his feet and clapped one of his hands onto theirs. His other hand slapped theirs from below. He grabbed a tight hold and, beaming widely, bounced their hands up and down.

He noticed the three men staring at him, waiting for him to finish.

Salmoneus hastily let go and stretched his smile to cover his embarrassment. None of the others smiled. Salmoneus dropped his smirk and wondered if there was a hole in this cavern that he could crawl into.

One of the sleeping soldiers moaned. Hercules turned; he hoped, *Don't wake up. I don't want to have to hit you again.* The man fell back into a silent sleep.

"Slaughterius," Hercules said quietly, "We've got to get out of here before our napping little children wake up."

"I agree, son," said the Pastoralian. "Do you have a plan?"

Hercules swept his gaze around the room. "As a matter of fact," he said slowly, a thought forming, "I just might."

He turned back to Slaughterius. "A while ago, you said we should keep quiet because there were guards outside. Where?"

Slaughterius led his two guests to a dark hole in the wall, tall and wide enough for a man. "This is

124

the mouth of a tunnel," Slaughterius whispered as he led Hercules, Salmoneus, and Cactus inside. "At the end is a door. It has a nasty drawback, though: guards on the other side.

"Since they haven't come to rescue, replace, or relieve the soldiers in the cavern," Slaughterius whispered to Hercules, "I assume that the guards outside are under orders not to open the door until the guards here on the inside kill you. If the guards outside came inside, then you'd realize that there was an open door somewhere, and you might escape."

From behind them, the men heard a soft moan and the scraping sound of a man slowly pulling himself off of the rocky floor. "Uh, guys," Salmoneus said, "whatever we do, we'd better do it quick. Our dance partners back there are waking up."

Hercules agreed. *They'll hear us here,* he thought, *and then we'll be trapped—stuck between five guards behind us and Zeus alone knows how many on the other side of this door.*

He noticed Cactus leaning against the cave wall. *Poor guy; he must be exhausted. I can't count on him to fight like he did before.* He glanced at the others. *Slaughterius has guts and brains, but he's old and frail; how long can he hold out? And Salmoneus is as much use in a fight as a pound of feathers. No, feathers at least have sharp points. I've got to move on my own.*

And I don't know what to do.

13

Hercules examined the door. It felt much like the door in the pit where he had seen Dryope and the fake Slaughterius: layers of strong, polished metal, coated with slippery ooze and bonded to thick granite. Pounding through it would take an hour, if his knuckles could hold out.

And they didn't have an hour. He could hear the soldiers moaning and getting to their feet.

Hercules' fingers passed over the thin gap between the door and the cave wall. He pressed his ear to the gap; he could hear the soldiers on the other side gossiping, griping, whistling. At least four different voices were out there.

"Hercules," Salmoneus whispered in his ear, "the guards behind us are up now, all of them. If you're going to do something, do it quick."

Hercules waved Salmoneus, Cactus, and Slaughterius back to the tunnel wall. *Maybe the guards won't notice them right away,* he hoped.

Slaughterius, still weak from the battles in the cavern, stumbled and slipped. His head hit the rock floor, and his eyes closed. "Slaughterius!" Hercules cried.

"Hercules!" Salmoneus hissed. "What are you doing?" He glanced frantically back toward the cavern. "They'll hear you!"

"Salmoneus, I need your help. Slaughterius is in trouble." Hercules fell silent for a moment; he could hear Slaughterius' breathing, which was labored, slow and shallow.

As Salmoneus and Cactus knelt before Slaughterius, Hercules could hear the guards on the other side of the door laughing. *They can hear me,* he thought. *I don't think that's good.*

A hard, gruff voice came through the door. "If you think you can bluff us into opening the door with that old trick, you better think again. 'My cellmate's dying'—I tried that one the first time I got put in jail. It didn't open the door then, and it won't now." More laughter, louder and rougher.

No! Hercules wanted to rip the door from the wall and shove it down the man's throat. *I'm the only one here who's not a liar! An impostor says he's me. An impostor says he's Slaughterius. The Mercs lie about the Pasters, the Pasters lie about the Mercs. They're so used to lies, they think everyone's lying.*

But I'm not lying!

Slaughterius opened his eyes. *Just fainted,* Hercules thought. *Good.*

He heard footsteps from the cavern growing closer. "Herc," said Salmoneus, his voice almost quieter than a newborn's breath, "do something. The guys in the big chamber—they heard you. They're coming this way.

No response. Hercules was lost in thought. *They think everyone's lying. . . .*

"You don't understand!" Hercules shouted at the door.

"Herc!" Salmoneus hissed. "Are you nuts?" The footsteps grew louder. The soldiers were coming closer. "Why don't you just tell these guys, 'Hey, come get us and chop us into meatloaf'?"

Slaughterius shushed him. Hercules yelled at the door, "I can't get out of this place!" He pounded the door; it vibrated but did not bend or crack. Slippery oil dripped off his hands and slid down his wrists. "You see? It's a perfect trap!"

"I admit it!" Hercules bellowed at the door. "I'll never get out of here. Right now, your friends are coming to kill me and my friends."

He looked over his shoulder. Waving their clubs high, seven soldiers were sprinting toward Hercules, revenge burning in their eyes.

Seven? Hercules wondered. He counted again: the first two guards, the three archers, and two others. Hercules looked at Slaughterius, who was staring in confusion at the two extra men. *He didn't know*, Hercules realized. *They were probably hiding. Once they saw what we did to their friends, they waited until the others recovered, so they could all attack at once.*

Hercules turned back to the door. "Your prison is just too perfect!" he roared. *Come on, guys,* he thought. *You think I'm a liar. I just told you I can't get out of here. That's the truth, but if you think it's a lie, then you've got to—*

The door flung open, bumping against Hercules' nose. He backed up rapidly and flung out his arms to push Slaughterius, Salmoneus, and Cactus against the wall. Salmoneus winced as cold goo slithered through his toga and onto his back.

Seven soldiers shot through the door and into the tunnel, led by a muscular man wearing a blue sash and wielding a club studded with gravel. *Captain Vicius,* Hercules realized.

The men from beyond the door were big, thick-necked former butchers and rangers, specially selected for bad tempers and mean methods, trained and drilled and fearless. Their clubs were sharpened, spiked, poisoned, pointed, pronged, and spurred. They sprinted forward, ready and eager to kill.

Too late, they noticed that they were about to collide with seven equally rough, well-armed men who were running toward them.

Vicius tried to slow down; so did the guard leading the group from the cavern. They jammed their heels into the rocky ground, braking hard. The guards behind them, caught unaware, rammed into the leaders' backs, knocked them face down onto the rocky floor, and spilled over them. Guards from the cavern landed on the heads of guards from the door, and more guards from the door crashed into the backs of more guards from the cavern.

Hercules grabbed Slaughterius and Salmoneus by the wrists. As the guards began pulling their arms and legs out of each other's way, Hercules yanked the peddler and the civic leader out from behind the door. As the guards scrambled to their feet, they saw him toss their former prisoners through the doorway and out of sight. Silently, Hercules wished his friends a soft landing and a clean escape.

Cactus stood near Hercules, guarding him as the soldiers rose. Hercules shoved the giant through the door and yelled, "Get out of here!" Cactus reluctantly obeyed.

Hercules was alone now, with both teams of guards ready to murder him.

Pain was pounding in Hercules' leg wound. Bruises throbbed in his back and chest from collisions with the pit floor and dungeon walls; cuts from rocks and sharp points stabbed throughout his body. His skin was tender and burning from exposure to acid. His muscles and bones were weary from fighting; his belly ached with hunger; his mouth was so dry that he felt his tongue might crack; he suddenly needed to find a bathroom; and he was mightily sick of people trying to kill him.

"Stay away from me, guys," Hercules said. "This'll hurt you more than it does me."

"He's lying," Vicius yelled. "Get him!" They rushed him, pounding forward at full speed with weapons high.

Hercules stepped behind the thick, heavy door and closed it in their faces. Unable to stop, they plowed into the hard, metal surface.

"Sorry, guys," Hercules murmured as he held the door closed with his back and shoulders. "You really ought to believe it when people tell you the truth."

Hercules turned serious. *Those guys may be stunned now*, he thought, *but they won't stay that way for long*.

He thought of the soldiers barreling through the door and flattening him under it.

Hercules looked forward; he was alone. The tunnel, lined with torches, quickly curved out of sight. No doubt Cactus had raced down the tunnel, looking for Slaughterius and Salmoneus. *If those big apes back there get into this tunnel*, he thought, *they'll find my friends*. He thought of Slaughterius and Salmoneus, weak and tired, trampled by the brawny horde.

He looked around. *There's gotta be a lock or some other way to keep those guys from pounding this door down*.

Hercules turned and examined the door. Two wide metal hinges clamped it to the wall. Two rusty iron sculptures in the shape of begging hands protruded from the door's surface.

Hercules looked to the side. There was a wide-open human mouth sculpted into the tunnel wall at the same level as the iron hands. He glanced at the opposite wall, and saw another open mouth at the hands' height. An iron bar, with finger grooves carved into it for easy gripping, poked out of the mouth.

Slide the bar through the hands and into the other wall's mouth, he thought, *so it pokes into both walls, and the only way anyone can open the door from inside the cavern is to push the door hard enough to shove the bar through two walls' worth of solid rock*.

Or bend the bar in trying. Even those husky guards, ramming repeatedly with all their weight and strength, might take an hour or more to do that.

Perfect, he thought. *The others'll be safe.* He wrapped his fingers around the bar, slipping his fingers into its cool, smooth ridges, and pulled. It was stuck; he pulled harder.

The bar suddenly came loose—but not all of it. Hercules found himself holding a four-foot shaft with a rough wedge of rock around one end. By trying to pull it out of the wall, he had pulled the bar apart and taken some of the wall with it.

Hercules turned the bar over to find out what had gone wrong. Near the rock wedge, the bar's tip looked partly like melted wax and partly like the squared-off tumblers of a complex lock. He looked in the hole from which he had pulled the shaft; he could make out the glint of torchlight reflecting off similar tumblers, some of which poked directly into the rock atop the hole.

A lock, he thought. *The stupid bar has a lock. I'd have to turn the thing in some weird combination— half a turn left, a full turn right, and a quarter-turn left or something—to pull it out safely. They probably put the lock there to keep people like me from doing things like . . . well, like trapping the guards. Hid the lock there to keep me from seeing it—*

A sudden, hot flush of anger welled up in Hercules' gut. *Can't these people be open about* anything? *All this hiding and faking and rotten tricks—*

A thunderous pounding hit the door from the inside, shaking it.

They're going to get through, Hercules thought. Since the door opened into the cavern, and since it had no handle inside the cavern to grab, there was only one way for the soldiers to open it: brute pounding.

A deep, heavy boom. The door seemed to jump toward Hercules. Flecks of rock shook off it and settled to the ground.

Hercules took the iron bar in both hands and swung it like a club, testing its weight. He touched the edge of the conical rock wedge. Heavy, craggy, and hard, it could easily punch a man's head off and pound the rest of his body to a red, squishy pulp.

Another blow to the door, a harder one, and another. The door kicked the ground, bucking like a wild stallion fighting a rider.

I don't want to kill them, Hercules thought. The bar was heavy in his hands. *But I can't talk them out of killing me; they won't believe anything I say. And no matter how hard I hit them, they keep coming.*

I may have to kill them.

Another pounding. One more impact and the door would open. The soldiers would come roaring out.

Okay, thought Hercules. *I know what I have to do.*

The final blow hit the door like a cannonball, knocking it flat on the tunnel floor. Through the clouds of dust rising from the impact, the soldiers saw the iron bar lying on the ground and Hercules dashing down the tunnel and out of sight.

"Coward!" Captain Vicius shouted as he led the soldiers after the demigod. "The real Hercules is a hero, but you're a phony and a coward!''

The words echoed down the walls. *Wrong,* Hercules thought. *I'm trying to keep people alive, but you won't believe that.*

He flung himself around a corner and kept running. He was out of the men's sight, but not for long. He could hear the stampede of soldiers surging louder and nearer. *Salmoneus, Slaughterius, Cactus,* he thought, *where in the world are you? I've got to get you to safety!*

''Herc!'' came a whisper from behind him.

Hercules skidded to a halt, ripping his feet on the rocky floor. He turned and carefully crept back the way he had come. He looked from side to side, floor to ceiling, but saw no one.

''Salmoneus?'' he asked. The ground rumbled and vibrated as the guards' running boots hit the ground. They were charging hard and closing in.

''In here!'' the peddler whispered. A pale hand emerged from a shadowy niche in the wall and yanked on Hercules' shirt. Hercules pulled the hand off and sidled into the darkness.

The soldiers whipped around the corner and stormed past him. The vibrating subsided.

They'll be back, Hercules knew, poking his head out and watching them go. *It won't take them long to notice that I'm not ahead of them. Whatever I do now, I'd better do it quick.*

Arms grabbed him around the belly. A head bumped his back and burrowed in between his shoulder blades.

''Herc, you're okay!'' Salmoneus cried. He

squeezed his friend tight. "We weren't sure you'd make it. We've been waiting for—"

"Quiet," a voice whispered from out of the darkness. "Salmoneus, let him breathe." Salmoneus let go.

"Thanks, Slaughterius," Hercules said quietly. "Is Cactus with you?"

A short silence, then a familiar bass rumble: "I'm here."

Hercules felt tense muscles in his neck relax. He turned in the darkness to find his partners.

He appeared to be in a cave. It had no torches, but the edges of a few rocks caught the yellow glow of the torches in the tunnel outside.

"Slaughterius, you know these tunnels," Hercules called into the darkness. "Is there anyplace we can go? Those soldiers won't be gone forever."

"Follow me," Slaughterius' voice replied from deep within the cave. "Watch your step. We're in one of the newer tunnels that I was having built, and it's unfinished. The ground can be rough here."

Rougher than out there? Hercules wondered, the bottom of his foot touching the cold, rocky ground. His next step put him on slippery gravel.

He heard a thump and then a curse from Salmoneus. Before he could ask what was wrong, he bumped into the same thing that Salmoneus had: a wall. The tunnel had turned a corner in the blackness, but they'd kept going straight.

"Hercules," he heard Slaughterius say. "Walk toward my voice. I'm standing by a fork in the tunnel.

Come to me and stand at the point between the forks."

Hercules stepped forward. He felt the wall curve away from his fingers; the tunnel was turning. No, he realized; forking. He ran his hand through the air, feeling for the point.

The side of his pinky finger hit a wall. He ran his hand along it and grabbed something hard and cool and shaped like a sharp V. "Got the point," he said.

"Good," Slaughterius said. He seemed to be practically standing in Hercules' ear.

In the distance, Hercules could hear the footsteps of the guards. *They're coming back*, he thought.

Slaughterius heard the sounds, too. "We'll have to rush," he whispered. "Hercules, squat."

"What?" Hercules whispered. He hoped that his voice showed the exasperated expression that was twisting his face.

"Don't argue," said the voice in the dark. "Bend as low as you can. Your bottom should nearly touch the floor. Don't sit all the way down, though; the rocks there are sharper than knives."

Feeling like a fool, Hercules hunkered down. Bending so low stretched and tore the wound in his leg. He blinked back tears of pain.

A row of jagged rocks started to rake his bottom.

"Okay, I'm squatted," he whispered.

"Good," said Slaughterius. The soldiers' footsteps were getting louder. "Hold your wrists as low as you can; again, nearly touching the floor. Clasp your hands together, palms up, fingers laced. Your hands should be making a bowl."

Slaughterius, Hercules decided, was a natural leader. Giving orders changed him from an exhausted old man to a vigorous commander. Hercules obeyed him. "Done."

"Good. Lock your fingers tight. Brace yourself and tense your muscles; you're going to need them. Prepare to push up."

What's that supposed to mean? Hercules wondered.

Before he could ask, something firm, nearly flat and very heavy pushed his palms down, shoving his knuckles into the gravelly ground. As Hercules bit his lip to keep himself from yelling, another flat object, just as heavy, crunched his hands down harder. The objects shifted left and right, grinding his skin into the ground's sharp points and hard edges. By touch, Hercules recognized the items: human feet. Slaughterius' feet, no doubt.

"Okay, I'm set," Slaughterius said softly. "Now, push me upward, fast!"

"Are you crazy?" Hercules asked. "I can't do that. I'll squash you against the ceiling. You'll be flatter than a slice of bread."

"I can hear them!" Vicius' harsh voice called from the shallow end of the tunnel. Cactus and Salmoneus turned toward it. "We've found them," Vicius barked. Hercules could hear him running. "Follow me!"

"Hercules," Slaughterius hissed between gritted teeth, "There's no time to argue. I know what I'm doing. Lift, you dolt. Lift!"

If he had had time, Hercules would have shrugged.

See you in the underworld, he thought. He heaved the Pastoralian skyward.

The man's weight left Hercules' hands. Hercules heard the slap of Slaughterius' palms hitting a rock surface and a grunt and scramble as Slaughterius pulled himself upward.

From the blackness overhead came Slaughterius' voice: "Hercules, squat down again and keep your hands in the same position. Salmoneus, it's your turn. Step forward till you feel Hercules' hands under your feet."

Hercules could hear the sound of fast-running boots approaching from the tunnel's mouth. "Move!" Slaughterius finished.

Two more feet pushed Hercules' knuckles onto the rocks. Again, he thrust his hands up high, and again the weight flew up from his fingers.

He heard what he hoped was Slaughterius' hand clamp onto Salmoneus' arm; Salmoneus scuffled and grunted as Slaughterius pulled him up to wherever Slaughterius was.

"Hercules, Cactus," Slaughterius commanded. "There's a hole in the ceiling of the tunnel you're in. Jump straight up, about eight feet. Go more than ten feet and you'll split your skull on the ceiling of the tunnel above you, the tunnel I'm in. Jump!"

The two big men bent and sprang. As he rose, Hercules could feel the cool air from above brushing his sweaty arms. His hand grazed the ceiling of the tunnel.

Hands grabbed his torso and jerked him forward. He rolled onto a pair of bodies and then onto a surface, soft but knobby. The surface moved; it was a man's chest. A bony hand—Slaughterius', he was sure—covered his mouth to keep him quiet.

"The seven of you!" called Vicius' raspy voice. "Search the tunnel forking to the left. The rest of you, come with me; we'll take the other tunnel. Wherever that lowlife fraud goes, we're going to catch him. Get your butts moving!"

Hercules heard the scuffling of boots and the occasional curse fade into the distance. Soon, the sounds diminished; even the echoes were gone. Hercules let out a long breath and was surprised at it; he hadn't realized until now that he had been holding his breath for quite a long time.

"Slaughterius?" He tossed the word softly into the dark and hoped that he was facing the right way. "Can you get us out of here?"

"Certainly." The civic leader's familiar voice floated up from behind Hercules. "Follow me. It won't be far."

The men got to their feet. Hercules could hear Slaughterius padding forward and walked toward the sound.

The stone floor was hard, smooth, and on a slight incline. "I'm sorry that I had to be so rude with you," Slaughterius went on. "With all of you. But those guards were approaching, and there was no time to ask permission and make explanations."

He sounded sincere. Hercules said, "No problem. We know how it is. Where are we going?"

"And are we safe?" Salmoneus asked, his voice trembling slightly.

Hercules could hear Slaughterius chuckling. "Certainly we're safe. Oh, there's a chance that those soldiers may find us, or that other soldiers may be patrolling this tunnel, but this tunnel isn't very well known. I built it as an escape route in case I ever had to flee the city." Hercules nodded, realizing even as he was doing it that Slaughterius couldn't see him. "Slow down," Slaughterius ordered.

Hercules slowed. He heard Slaughterius' hands patting the wall as he moved forward. Before he could ask what the man was doing, he heard Slaughterius stop patting. "Ah, here we are," the old man announced. "Stop, please."

Hercules halted. He heard Slaughterius stamp his foot three times on the tunnel floor. A section of the tunnel wall slid upward, stopping only when it became flush with the ceiling.

Golden light burst into the tunnel. Hercules raised a hand to shield his eyes from the glow.

"Come on," Slaughterius ordered. "It gets easier now."

Hercules squinted and blinked; his eyes adjusted to the light. He was looking at a flight of stairs carved into solid rock, with torches lining the walls on both sides.

Salmoneus sneezed. "Sorry," he said. "That breeze tickled my nose hairs—hey, wait a second. A breeze?"

Hercules could feel it, too: a cool breeze sliding from the top of the stairs. *We're getting close to the outside*, he thought.

Slaughterius stamped his feet again. The door slid

down the tunnel wall, closing it off. "Let's go," he said.

They began climbing the stairs, with Slaughterius in the lead. "In case you're wondering," Slaughterius went on, "some of the tunnel doors work on a counterweight system. Many of these walls and floors are hollow, you see. When I stamped my feet, I tripped a trigger tied to a slab inside the walls. The slab is connected by rope and pulley to the door. Now, the slab's a little heavier than the door, so when the trigger dropped out from under the slab—"

"The slab dropped and pulled the door up," Hercules finished. "And when you needed to close the door, you just stamped again." *Hmmm*, he mused. *That explains how the people we chased from the surface down here got out of the pit, and we couldn't. They knew how to raise the door—and we didn't.*

Slaughterius was taking two steps at a time now, with Hercules behind him. Hercules glanced over his shoulder to make sure that Salmoneus and Cactus were all right.

He saw the giant carrying Salmoneus. Hercules scowled—the smaller man was taking advantage of the giant's strength and innocence—but the peddler only shrugged. "He offered to carry me," he said.

"Cactus, please put him down," Hercules said mildly. "Salmoneus, you can walk. Look at Slaughterius."

Slaughterius was jogging briskly up the stairs, wheezing but intrepid. "We'll be on the surface soon," he said, looking over his shoulder. He picked up the pace to a full run. "This stairway brings us up behind one of the city walls, the wall that faces Mercantilius." He began leaping three stairs at a time.

Hercules sprinted alongside him. *You really do want out, don't you?* he thought. Slaughterius was leaning toward the top, his body at a forward tilt, his legs pumping, neck muscles stretched and straining, sweat dripping off his brow.

The old man picked up his pace and sped upward. *Slaughterius*, Hercules thought, *you could give Hermes a run for his money.*

He glanced over his shoulder and found Salmoneus and Cactus not far behind. Although Salmoneus was lagging, Cactus was pulling the peddler's hand and trying to drag him upward. Salmoneus was protesting—begging, actually—but climbing.

Slaughterius stopped. They had reached the top.

Hercules looked up. The ceiling was a square covered in dark mahogany planks laid in a crisscross pattern for maximum strength. As Cactus, Slaughterius, and Salmoneus watched, Hercules laid a hand on the planks and slowly pushed upward.

The ceiling angled out, creaking. Its edges were fringed in thin, fragile leaves that Hercules recognized as blades of grass. *A checkerboard square*, he realized. *Of course.*

The night sky was clear and full of bright stars. A cool breeze floated along, teasing Hercules' hair. He stepped out of the checkerboard square, with Slaughterius, Salmoneus, and Cactus following. Cactus gently closed the square behind them.

Hercules dropped to his hands and knees, and lowered himself until he was belly-down on the grass. "Everybody, drop," he said. "We've got to move, but I don't want us to walk upright; there's no shelter, and we've got to do anything we can not to get spotted."

He looked around as the others lay on the grass. He saw a city wall not far to his left, and another not far to his right. The dark gap between the walls stood dead ahead.

"You were right, Slaughterius," he whispered. "We're pretty close to one of the ways out of here." There were no guards in sight, but the Pastoralians were quick and clever; guards might spring out at any moment.

Hercules began slithering forward like a snake and waved for the others to follow. He began plotting strategy. *The Mercantilians are supposed to attack at dawn, and the fake Slaughterius knows it. So he'll probably attack before dawn.*

But how long before dawn?

Probably an hour or two, while the Mercantilians are still in bed. He probably won't attack much earlier than that, because his own troops need their sleep. To no one in particular, he muttered, "I just wish I knew what time it is."

"Telling time? That's not difficult," Slaughterius said. His voice sounded puny, like something rustling in the far distance. "Just let me read the stars." He looked up; Hercules could hear the bones in the old man's neck crackle.

"Mmmm . . . yes . . . well," Slaughterius mumbled. "Aha!" More crackling noises as the old man lowered his head. "We're about four hours before dawn."

Hercules sighed and smiled. He let his face rest on the cool, dewy grass. *Whew! I've got time.*

Filled with hope and renewed energy, he began slithering forward again, faster than before. He ignored Salmoneus' whiny "Hey, Herc, wait up!" and kept going.

He reached the gap and peered into it. He saw only darkness in the shadows that the tall wall cast; he heard no sounds except the soft shuffle and swish of the others slipping through the grass behind him.

Hercules grabbed the edge of the nearer wall and pulled himself to his feet. He took inventory of his pains from his feet on up, but they were too many to keep in his mind at one time; he stopped at the burning acid hole at his hip and the rock scars on his thighs.

If I don't get this mission wrapped up fast, he thought, *I'll find out whether I'm as immortal as my father or as mortal as my mother. This whole affair is going to kill me.* He smiled grimly. *I never thought that stopping a war could make a man die.*

The rustling behind him stopped as Cactus helped Slaughterius and Salmoneus to their feet. "Thanks," Hercules told the giant. "Let's go."

They slipped through the gap and found themselves in the corridor that ran between the walls. Lifting their feet only an inch into the air and placing them on the rocky floor slowly and carefully, like a mother laying her newborn baby in a crib, they managed to stay silent. Inch by inch, as slowly as if they were walking through molasses, they moved forward through the darkness.

Hercules could see dark blue ahead. The night sky seemed to be waiting for them. Guards would be waiting, too, he knew.

He turned his head and caught Cactus' eye; the giant tiptoed forward. Hercules forced himself not to smile at the sight of the broad-shouldered, thick-chested, cannon-armed behemoth trying to move with lightness and delicacy.

When Cactus arrived, Hercules pulled the giant's head close to his own. "See that opening with the staircase up ahead?" he whispered. Cactus nodded slowly. "There's a guard station with at least four armed soldiers at the top. Beyond the guard station is a thirty-foot drop. We'll have to hit them fast and hard—but we'll have to be careful, or we could go falling. Are you with me?"

Cactus looked at the blue gap for a very long time. Hercules tried not to be impatient, and simply let the man study.

Cactus' gaze returned to Hercules. "I'm with you," he answered, his voice low and sure.

Hercules started to clap the man's shoulder, but he pulled back; slapping a man on bruises like Cactus' would hurt like throwing him into a blazing furnace. He settled for shaking Cactus' hand. "Let's go," he told the giant.

They crept forward into the darkness between the walls, Hercules listening like a cat for any sounds of the guards. He heard nothing, which bothered him. *Do they know we're coming? Are they waiting for us?*

He glanced at Cactus, who stared resolutely forward. *If there's trouble, how do I tell him about it without them hearing it? And what do I tell him to do about it?*

He saw no choice but to keep moving forward.

They reached the edge of the staircase close to the guard station. Hercules backed up against one wall. Cactus followed his lead and laid his back against the other. He looked at Hercules, waiting for a signal.

Hercules turned his head; he couldn't see Slaughterius and Salmoneus in the shadowy pathway, but he saw their eyes shining, reflecting the starlight. They seemed to be huddling close to each other—at least, Hercules thought wryly, Salmoneus was huddling— and waiting for Hercules to move.

Hercules reached up. The wall felt rough; he remembered that it was made of hundreds of small stones mortared into place. He scratched the wall with his fingernails until a few pebbles cascaded down his fingers and into his palm.

He threw them onto the floor. They rattled in the otherwise silent night air.

Hercules glanced to the opening. *Well?* he thought. *I just gave you guys a noise; it proves there's someone here. Come investigate so Cactus and I can clobber you!*

No one appeared. *They're on to me,* he thought. *I'll have to do this the hard way.*

He gripped the edge of the wall and swung around the corner feet first and legs high, shrieking like a maniac, hoping to kick a guard's gut while scaring the guard's partners. Cactus followed, leaping from

147

the other wall, offering his own whoops and screams.

But the guard post was deserted. It took Hercules only a second to figure out why. He turned to call back down the stairs.

"Come on, guys, it's all right."

Slaughterius reached the edge of the wall and rounded the corner. Hercules couldn't see his expression, but the man's gasp told him all he needed to know.

Salmoneus stepped forward. He clenched his teeth to keep them from chattering, though Hercules couldn't tell if it was a reaction to the elements or to emotion.

"Hey," he asked, "where'd the beefy boys go?" He looked at Hercules and Cactus. "Present company excepted."

Slaughterius and Cactus were staring over the railing. Hercules looked at Salmoneus and turned to stare outward as well. He pointed down at the forested lands below. "There they are," he said.

Salmoneus looked. He reeled and nearly fainted.

One thousand armed Mercantilians, massed in a tight, square formation, were marching from their city toward the high ridge that separated Mercantilius from Pastoralis. One thousand armed Pastoralians, arranged in a triangle at the base of their city walls, were marching into the forest toward the same ridge.

Salmoneus turned to Hercules, confused. "What happened?"

"They lied," Hercules said darkly. He squeezed the railing tight and had to stop himself from crushing it. "The Mercantilians said they'd attack at dawn, but they're attacking now."

He looked up. *Ares, you monster. You set this up. All those people are going to die, and for what?*

"Can you stop them?" Cactus asked Hercules. He looked worried and suddenly smaller.

Hercules frantically sifted through plans in his mind. "I don't know," he said.

"I do," called a familiar voice behind him.

The four men slowly turned. In the gap between the walls stood Captain Vicius and several other soldiers, all aiming arrows at Hercules and his colleagues.

14

"Hercules," said Cactus, "look." The giant was pointing at the pathway cut into the wall leading to the guard station. In the pathway stood more guards, also aiming at the men's hearts.

"I hate to say this, Hercules," Slaughterius said, "but there, too." He pointed lower. On the ladder cut into the wall, leading from the pathway to the ground, stood more sharpshooters.

"Uh, Herc?" Salmoneus said. Hercules turned. Salmoneus was facing the wall on the other side of the guard platform. The wall had its own pathway and ladder, which had their own guards taking aim at him.

There were more than forty guards in all—and they, Hercules realized, were only the ones he could see. How many more were in hiding, ready to attack, like the archers in the cavern?

"One twitch," said Vicius, "and you and your friends are pincushions."

Hercules' brain raced. Without moving anything but his eyes, he traced the few feet between himself and Vicius. *Can I jump him? Maybe.*

He looked at the soldiers lined up at Vicius' sides and behind him. They were young, sharp-eyed, probably quick and eager to react. *If I make a move, it'll trigger his men to open fire.* Hercules could feel Salmoneus, Cactus, and Slaughterius watching him. *I might find a way to survive. But what about the others?*

He risked a fast glance over the guard station's railing. The armies were on the march toward each other. *I've got to do something. Those men will kill each other.*

Vicius sneered at Hercules. "You think you're so smart. Once you lost us in the tunnels, I decided there was only one place you would go: out. All I had to do was alert my lieutenants to cover the city's exits."

Vicius stopped sneering; his gaze turned hard as ice. "Coward," Vicius said, his voice saturated with contempt. "Running like a scared jackrabbit. And you call yourself *Hercules*."

He wants us dead, Hercules thought. *I can see it. He's tried to kill us, but we humiliated him, so he must want to kill us—to kill me—more than ever.*

He can do it, too. All he has to do is tell his men to fire.

So why hasn't he done it? Why is he talking to me? Someone must have ordered him not to kill us.

Vicius stepped forward. "Come with me," he ordered his prisoners. "Men, follow me," he said to the guards.

The captain took his captives back between the walls, leading them toward the city. *What's he doing?* Hercules wondered.

"Get out," Vicius said quietly. Only the four prisoners could hear him.

"What?" Hercules asked softly as he kept walking.

"I mean it," Vicius whispered. "You outdid me down in those tunnels. I respect that. No one's ever done it before. So just get out of here and never let me see you again."

Confusion washed over Hercules. *Is he lying? Or does he really have a sense of honor? The Pastoralians were honorable people before the war; why not during it?*

"Go!" Vicius said quietly. "You have ten seconds. Nine. Eight. Six."

"Hey!" Salmoneus shouted. "What happened to seven?"

He wants us gone fast, Hercules thought. *I understand him now.*

He stopped walking.

"We surrender," Hercules said, loud enough for the soldiers behind Vicius to hear.

Salmoneus stared at him, wide-eyed. "We do?"

"Halt!" Vicius called to his guards.

"You're lying," he told Hercules, barely holding back an explosion of fury, "but I got my orders." He turned to a soldier standing just behind his right shoulder. "Spread the word. We're taking them to the general."

He shifted his gaze back to Hercules. "All right, you. And the other three." He swung his bow and arrow toward the path in the wall behind Hercules and his allies. "Start marching down that pathway." He seemed very grumpy.

Poked by arrows, Hercules, Salmoneus, Slaughterius, and Cactus began to march toward the walkway. Salmoneus stepped up next to Hercules and whispered, "What was that all about?"

A pink-faced soldier came trotting up from behind Vicius. No older than fourteen, the boy carried a roll of parchment and a long, white quill whose tip was stained a shiny black. The boy saluted briskly and said in a high, piping voice with just a hint of a tremble, "Captain Vicius, sir! Begging the captain's pardon, sir, but according to regulations, sir, now that the prisoners are captured, sir, the captain has to make a report on his earlier failures to capture the—"

Vicius pulled out the club strapped to his hip and slashed the boy across the face. The boy went down and hit the floor, out like a snuffed candle. The troops behind Vicius curved around the boy as they followed their captain along the walkway.

Without turning around, Vicius growled, "Trample him."

"That's what that was all about," Hercules softly told Salmoneus. "He's furious because he failed. Because we made him fail, and he'd have to tell his commander. He wants us dead."

Salmoneus shrugged. "So why'd he let us go?"

"He didn't," Hercules replied. "He wanted us to *think* he was letting us go. What happens when prisoners escape?"

Salmoneus thought hard. "The soldiers try to catch them."

Hercules nodded. "What if they can't catch them?"

A light dawned in Salmoneus' head. "They shoot them. He was setting us up to be killed."

"Exactly," Hercules said. "He's got orders to take us to his general, but he'd rather see us dead. So he tried to arrange our deaths in a way the general would allow. He wanted us to give him an excuse to let his men shoot us."

"Yeah, but how'd you know, Herc?" Salmoneus asked.

"It was that ten-second count," Hercules answered. "I figured if he'd lie about that, he was lying about that offer to let us run away. So the best way to stay alive was not to run away. It was to surrender."

Vicius banged the back of Hercules' head with his club. Hercules tried to roll with the blow, but his head throbbed nevertheless. "Shut up, you!" the captain commanded.

Hercules didn't mind. *Shout all you want, Captain Toughguy,* he thought. *I've got liars like you figured out.*

Not much later, Hercules and his friends had marched along the wall's stone walkway and crawled down the ladder. They stood between the wall and the woods, unable to see.

Hercules was raising his opinion of Vicius. The soldier may not always have shown skill at improvising his way through unexpected problems, but at carrying out specific plans and orders he was flawless. Well before Hercules' party had touched the ground, Vicius had ordered them blindfolded; with startling swiftness, the captain had stationed a soldier behind every nearby tree. He sent other soldiers to the edges of the route that he had planned for the four prisoners to take through the forest.

When Vicius had the blindfolds removed, he marched double-quick into the forest and ordered the prisoners to keep up with him. He demanded that they look straight ahead, and had his soldiers pull the prisoners' ears whenever they looked to the side. The punishment was surprisingly painful and very effective.

A light breeze rustled the leaves and brushed a few strands of Hercules' hair into his face. As he waved them away, his hand shielded his face from Vicius' view. He glanced around quickly, taking in everything he could see in the starlight.

From every direction, he saw arrows pointed at himself and his three colleagues. If they chose to flee, they would run into bowmen, and more beyond them. As they moved through the forest, the mass of soldiers sped silently from tree to tree, moving with them like a school of sharks circling a drowning man, surrounding him wherever he went as he moved through the ocean waves.

Vicius' club poked Hercules in the belly. Its sharp points stung. "Put the hand down," the captain demanded.

Hercules let his arm drop back to his side and stared straight ahead, hoping to see holes in Vicius' troop deployment. He couldn't find any.

The group was marching up the long rise that separated Pastoralis from Mercantilius. As he pressed on, Hercules' bare feet felt dents in the soft soil. He heard the boots of the Pastoralian army ahead of him, marching in a tight, fast rhythm, punching the patterns of their boot soles into the softened ground like a multitude of hammers beating a sheet of metal into submission.

From what he had seen at the guard station, Hercules was sure that even as the Pastoralian army was heading up the rise toward Mercantilius, the Mercantilian army was heading up the other side toward Pastoralis. From the fast pace of the Pastoralian bootsteps, he estimated that he had less than half an hour before the armies would meet atop the rise and start to destroy each other.

No one's going to win, he realized. The armies seemed so evenly matched that neither side could defeat the other. Two thousand men would die bloodily with no result except pain and mourning.

Up ahead, through the trees, he not only could hear men but was starting to see some of them. Vicius' group was gaining on the rest of the army.

The rear guard of the armed forces was a solid row of soldiers, shoulder to shoulder. A leather cap covered each man's skull from his forehead all the way back to the top of his spine and from ear to ear. Leather boots protected the men's feet.

Every man wore an armored vest from his shoulder to his hips. Strapped to the back of the vest were a bow and a quiver of arrows. Strapped to each thigh was a holster carrying a club that each had customized to his particular taste in murder: sharp points, poisoned tips, hard edges, flammable coatings, and more.

Some of the men, apparently specialists, had other weapons. One had a sling slipped around his shoulder. A whip coiled around the arm of another. Yet another had nailed leather pockets to his armor; in the pockets he had knives of various lengths.

There were more soldiers than Hercules could take in. The line seemed endless, stretching further than he could see without turning his head.

Vicius jabbed Hercules with his club. "Turn right. Run," he commanded. Hercules swallowed his anger and, following Vicius, began a slow trot, just slightly faster than a quick march. He could hear the other prisoners and guards jogging behind him.

They passed the end of the army's back row of soldiers. "Left," Vicius commanded, and Hercules turned. As he ran, Hercules' head bobbed, allowing him quick, corner-of-the-eye glimpses of the troops they were passing.

In the starlight, dappled into a patchwork by the shadows of trees and leaves, Hercules saw marching infantrymen, mounted cavalrymen, heavily laden weapons bearers, swift-darting perimeter scouts, and a dozen other types of soldiers. He tried to count the rows of men; he found well over forty.

A few of the younger soldiers turned to look at the strange crew running uphill past them. Their heads immediately snapped forward as they remembered that their job was to march, not to stare.

Pretty darn disciplined for a city of shepherds, Hercules thought. *When these guys actually get into a fight, they'll be terrifying.* He didn't like the idea.

Hercules noticed that the rows of soldiers were getting shorter as he ascended the ridge. The last row seemed to have fifty men, the second-to-last had forty-nine, the next had forty-eight, and so on. Now, he saw, they were passing rows of less than a dozen men apiece, with fewer in each succeeding line.

Hercules remembered that from the guard station, he saw that the troops were arranged in a big triangle, with the point leading the rest toward Mercantilius. *We're getting toward the front,* he thought.

Finally, as they neared the top of the rise, they passed a row of only two men. Like Vicius, they wore shoulder-to-hip sashes, but while his was a captain's blue, theirs were shining silver. Hercules had no doubt that the color signified a rank far higher than Vicius'.

Above and beyond the two silver soldiers, well ahead of the rest of the advancing troops, four common soldiers held the four posts of a tall tent of golden silk. The men marched in synch to keep the tent a perfect square with a taut top, its walls hanging almost to the ground. The front wall was swept back onto the tent's roof, allowing the tent's occupants to see where they were going.

Following Vicius, Hercules pulled even with the tent. To pick up a clue as to the tent's contents, he glanced down at the gap between the tent's hem and the ground.

He saw the legs of a horse. *They can't be protecting just a horse from the cold night air,* he told himself.

He looked again. He saw a pair of sandaled feet jogging alongside the horse. The fact struck him as strange. The tent was enormous, wider and longer than most houses; why reserve that much space for one man and one horse?

The sharp edges of Vicius' club raked Hercules' chest. "Eyes front," he growled. "Turn left. We're going into the tent."

Following Vicius, Hercules jogged toward a slit in one of the tent's side walls. As the men holding the tent posts ran, the cloth hanging on either side of the slit bounced and flapped, giving Hercules glimpses of the inside. He couldn't see the face of the person on the horse, but he noted that the man wore satin leggings of sunrise gold and soft, well-polished leather boots.

He passed through a slit in the tent's wall. Inside the tent, he saw that the horse was an enormous palomino. A man was jogging beside her, as thin as a pencil, his skin and hair as white as milk.

The jogger, a short man, was holding his arms almost straight up, presenting a tray of tiny chocolates to the man in the horse's smooth, burgundy-leather saddle.

The man atop the horse wore a gleaming golden vest, a silk blouse of matching gold, and had no club or bow and arrow. With his boots and golden leggings, he looked like a lemon in shoes.

Still running to keep up with the tent's uphill advance, Hercules recognized the horseman's face. Before he could speak to the man, however, the rest of the prisoners and guards began flowing in through the flap, crowding the inside of the tent.

To avoid the crowd, Hercules sped up his pace and ran to the front wall of the tent. He turned and, running backward, looked up at the horse's rider.

"Hello, 'Slaughterius,' " he said, with an edge of contempt in his voice.

"Why, isn't this nice," said the impostor. "Hello, again, clown." He looked around and saw Cactus and Salmoneus. "And I see you've brought friends. How lovely!"

The real Slaughterius hobbled into the tent. "Oh. You again," sneered the phony. "Well, I'll deal with *you* later."

He caught Cactus' eye and waved him forward. Cactus jogged side by side with Hercules. "My, my . . . *two* of you big boys. Remarkable. You must be formidable in a fight."

"Slaughterius" glanced over Hercules' shoulder and out the open front of the tent. *What's he looking at?* Hercules wondered. Still running uphill and backward, he glanced over his shoulder and tried to focus on the sights despite his awkward posture and bobbing body.

He realized that he looked ridiculous. He ignored the feeling and tried to see what "Slaughterius" found so fascinating.

"Halt!" the phony Slaughterius yelled.

Instantly, the tent holders stopped running, and the tent held still. Hercules nearly fell over as he braked. He could hear the two men at the head of the pyramid of troops shouting "Halt!" and other officers down the rows of men repeating the order to their subordinates.

The phony Slaughterius swung a leg over his saddle, sitting sideways on the horse's back. The servant who had been presenting him with candies immediately set the tray on the ground and dropped to his hands and knees.

The phony slid out of the saddle and landed, feet first, on the servant's back. The servant sagged in the middle and winced in pain, but stayed steady. Standing on the man's back, "Slaughterius" surveyed the scene. He appeared to enjoy standing well above the others around him.

"Slaughterius" pointed a limp finger at Salmoneus and the real Slaughterius. "Take those two back to the city," he told Vicius.

Hercules opened his mouth to object, but Slaughterius spoke first. "Don't worry, Hercules. We'll be all right. With a war on the way, we're probably safest behind the city walls."

The captain nodded at the guards surrounding the peddler and the politician. They herded the men out as if leading pigs to a pen, striking their legs occasionally to get them out fast. Vicius and a dozen other guards stayed to keep an eye on Hercules and Cactus.

"Slaughterius" stepped down from the back of his servant, who sighed gratefully. The general paced in a circle around Hercules and Cactus, eyeing their muscles. He approached them from behind, wedged himself between them and slung his arms over their shoulders.

"Now, tell me," he trilled, "why don't you join my side? With you two working for me, I could easily wipe out the Mercantilians."

Hercules pulled the man's arm off; Cactus did the same. "Listen to me," Hercules said urgently. "You can't wipe them out. You and the Mercs are too evenly matched. If you fight them, you'll only get your own troops hurt." He paused and tried to catch the general's eye. "But you don't have to fight them."

Hercules was not used to making speeches. Still, he poured all of his passion into this one.

The Pastoralian and the Mercantilian armies would destroy each other, Hercules said. Then the dead men's loved ones would vow revenge. He had seen plenty of wars, and that's the way that they always worked.

Needing fresh soldiers and supplies, the Mercantilians and Pastoralians would force citizens from other, smaller towns to choose sides and fight. The entire island of Peloponnesus would become a battlefield.

Other nations and city-states would avoid the dangerous island. So would businesses. No food, clothing, building supplies, or other necessities would replace the ones that the war would destroy. Children would starve or freeze to death. Hercules thought of Peuris and imagined the boy lying in a trench, washed in his own blood, his belly sunken from hunger, his arms too weak to raise a spear to defend himself against a marauder like Vicius.

And when the fighting finally ended, Hercules said, when enough people got sick enough of destruction and feuding, the pain would go on. The Peloponnesians would face years of poverty as they tried to rebuild their burned-out cities and revive their ravaged farms.

Even worse, they would never again trust people from other towns. Mercantilians would tell horror stories of the demonic monsters who lived in Pastoralis and killed the Mercantilians' parents. Pastoralians would tell the same stories about the Mercantilians. Sooner or later, war would flare up again. Generations of death and fire and agony and hatred and—

"That's . . . that's not true," said the impostor calling himself Slaughterius. He couldn't face Hercules, and one of his hands was shaking. His face had gone bone white. "You—you're lying." He grabbed Hercules by the shoulders and shook him. "You're lying!"

Behind Hercules, Vicius' soldiers looked at each other, worried. The only thing worse than a blood-thirsty military commander was an unpredictably crazy one. Vicius growled at the nervous guards to shut up, face front, and stand at attention.

"Slaughterius" looked at his hands, which were still clutching Hercules' shoulders. He let go, leaving long, pale imprints where his fingers had pressed into Hercules' flesh.

The general nervously ran his palms down the front of his breastplate, as if it were a shirt that he had wrinkled and needed to smooth. He stopped as he realized that he was trying to smooth beaten gold with his bare hands. For a moment, his hands hovered in midair; he reminded Hercules of a young teenage boy at his first dance, unsure of whether his hands belonged behind his back, at his sides, or inside his tunic.

"Slaughterius" dropped his hands to his sides; they hit his thighs with a dull slap that made him jump. Apparently he hadn't expected the sound. Rubbing his chin in deep thought, he turned away from Hercules.

He peered at the demigod out of the corner of his eye. "If," he began slowly, in a weak and quaking voice, "if I did want to stop this war . . . how would I go about it?"

In a deeper voice, he quickly added, "Not that I do want to stop it. You're lying about all that devastation and pain, of course. I don't believe a word of it."

His voice became gentler, less certain again. Even his eyes seemed softer, more doelike. "But if I did want to stop the war, what would I do?"

Hercules considered his reply carefully. "Well. . . . I would talk to Ferocius, the Merc general. He's in charge there. He's probably leading the troops now."

The Pastoralian grunted. "I see. I don't believe

you, of course, but—'' He closed his eyes and paced back and forth, mumbling to himself.

Hercules decided to take a risk. He leaned forward and spoke quietly into the ear of ''Slaughterius.'' ''I know what you're thinking,'' he said. ''You want to negotiate a peace settlement, but you don't know how. I know your city's history; you've never done anything like this before.

''Let me help you. I want you to get the peace you want.''

''Slaughterius' '' eyebrows shot up, but he did not admit that Hercules had stated any kind of truth. ''Nonsense!'' he shouted, too loudly and too fast.

Hercules held back a smile. *You're a liar*, he thought. *Just like Vicius back at the guard station. You're really scared of war. You just don't want to admit it, General Toughguy.*

Slaughterius calmed himself. ''Well, now, I have work to do.'' He turned to Hercules. ''And you, my man, are going to help me do it.'' He glanced at Cactus and then back at Hercules. ''This colossus—he is with you, is he not?''

Hercules nodded. ''That's right. He's saved my life more than once. I trust him the way I trust my right hand.''

Cactus smiled and blushed. *He really is some kind of overgrown kid,* Hercules thought.

''Good,'' the general allowed. ''I have a mission for you two. Servilius!''

''Down here, sir,'' squeaked the servant who had served ''Slaughterius'' his chocolates. He was still on his hands and knees, as he had been when ''Slaughterius'' slid off of the horse. Apparently, he didn't feel free to move unless "Slaughterius" ordered him to.

"Oh, do get up, Servilius," the general pouted. "Fetch me a quill and some parchment and my sealing wax. And get the blue bag from my luggage bearers."

The servant straightened up, parts of his body cracking and popping as he rose. He disappeared around the general's horse and quickly returned with a blank scroll, a long, ink-dipped feather, and a sky-blue sack tied shut with a drawstring.

"Slaughterius" took the parchment and pen from his servant, and turned his back. Hercules heard the pen scratching and resisted the temptation to look over the general's shoulder to see what he was writing.

The general turned back to Hercules and Cactus. He offered Hercules the scroll, now folded into fourths and sealed shut with wax. "Take this message to the leader of Mercantilius," he said. "You're not one of my soldiers; he may trust you." Hercules took the paper. "And don't read it!" the general squealed. "It's none of your business." Sighing, Hercules tucked the message into his belt.

"Now, for you," the general went on, taking the bag from his servant and handing it to Cactus, "you will give this to the Mercantilian leader as a—" He cut himself off. "Well, you'll give it to him," he finished curtly.

Hercules sniffed the air. A fresh, tart aroma was rising from the bag. "What's in there?" he asked.

"I told you," the general snapped. "None. Of. Your. Business!" He stepped toward Hercules, glaring into his eyes. "Is that clear?" Hercules didn't reply; he was still trying to identify the scent. *Some kind of plant*, he concluded. *What kind of plant would he want to send the Mercs?*

"Get going, both of you," the general ordered.

A rose would mean love, Hercules thought as he and Cactus approached the tent's front opening, *but I'm sure he doesn't love old General Ferocius.* In the background, he could hear "Slaughterius" yell, "Vicius!"

"Yes, sir!" the captain shouted, dashing to face his general. "Your orders, sir?"

"Position your archers at the front of my tent. Watch them as they go. If they head in any direction other than Mercantilius, shoot them." The general swept back to his horse. The servant dropped to his hands and knees.

Hercules heard the order and concluded that "Slaughterius" wanted him to hear it. The general was trying to scare his couriers into going in the right direction.

As Hercules and Cactus started climbing to the rise's tree-lined top, the son of Zeus went back to deducing the contents of Cactus' sack. *A lily means death*, Hercules thought. *An olive branch means peace—*

Hercules grinned. *It's a peace offering!* He fingered the paper in his belt. *I'll bet this is a message inviting Ferocius to make peace. No wonder he doesn't want me to see the plant or read the paper. That faker*

*would rather die than let me know that I've swayed
him from war to peace.*

Hercules and Cactus neared the top of the ridge.
Hercules looked over his shoulder and smiled at
"Slaughterius." *Gotcha, you old liar!* he thought. Vicius' archers trained their arrows at him; he didn't
care.

Then he noticed that the troops were starting to
rearrange themselves. The triangular formation of
their rows and columns was dissolving.

They were starting to form a semicircle, two arms
starting just below the top of the ridge and curving
inward to meet about a quarter of the way downhill.
It was, Hercules knew, a variation on a classic pincer
formation, perfect for ambushing anyone who might
come over the ridge.

His brow furrowed. *That's not the setup that a man
planning peace would order*, he thought. *Something's
wrong.*

Hercules heard a low buzzing. He glanced down at
the sack in Cactus' hand. Several flies were diving
toward the bag; others were soaring up to it. *The smell
must've attracted them,* Hercules thought.

He noticed one bug's flight path wavering. As it
approached the bag, the fly dipped and plunged, then
shakily rose a little, and finally dropped.

It plummeted to the ground, where it twitched for
a moment, then lay still. So did two more flies, and
then another three. Every fly getting within three feet
of the bag was dying.

Poison, Hercules realized. *That's no olive branch
in there. Whatever plant's in the bag, it's lethal.*

169

If Ferocius takes the plant out of the bag and holds it in his bare hands, it'll kill him.

He looked over his shoulder at "Slaughterius," who was grinning as he watched Hercules and Cactus approach the top of the rise. *All those hints that he really wanted peace—they were just an act.*

That liar's sending us to kill the leader of his enemies.

Once the Mercantilians see that we've killed their chief, they'll kill us. Hercules glanced at Cactus. *Cactus may be getting poisoned right now, just from holding the sack. I'd better tell him to drop it and run.*

As he opened his mouth, Hercules could hear Vicius telling one of his archers to watch his aim. *Drop it and run? That won't work. They'll shoot us both. But I've got to get Cactus away from that bag without letting those soldiers know I'm doing it.*

And I've got to do it fast.

Hercules snatched the sack out of Cactus' hands and screamed at him: "You traitor! You *liar!*"

Cactus looked as shocked as a man entering his home and seeing an elephant stampeding through his living room. He could not speak.

Hercules turned to the golden tent. "Did you hear what he just whispered?" he yelled at "Slaughterius." He whirled and pointed at the giant. "He said he wanted the Mercantilians *dead!*"

"Hercules," Cactus cried, "I did not! I—"

Hercules picked the giant up with both hands and threw him down at Vicius' archers, sending them tumbling into the tent flaps. "He wants to kill their leader, General Ferocius!'' Hercules shouted. ''Slaughterius, I know you want to make peace with Ferocius. Well, I'm going to make sure you do. I'm going to see the general myself—alone!''

He marched up the hillside. *That ought to do it,* he thought. *No matter what Cactus says, they'll believe that he wants the Mercantilians dead, just as they do. They'll think he's on their side. Cactus is safe.*

''Hercules?'' came the soft, musical tones of ''Slaughterius.''

Hercules turned and looked down at the Pastoralian. Cactus, he saw, was back on his feet.

''Slaughterius'' nodded at Vicius. Instantly, his archers shot Cactus full of arrows.

As the giant screamed and Hercules sprinted down to the tent, they fired again. Cactus collapsed.

Hercules swept the soldiers aside and cradled Cactus in his arms. The giant looked up at him, confusion and terror in his eyes.

''Hercules,'' he rasped, ''why did you lie?'' He coughed up blood. Hercules had no answer. Cactus coughed again, choked, and died.

Behind Hercules, ''Slaughterius'' chuckled. ''Oh, Hercules,'' he said, ''you poor fool. You should never try to deceive the master of deception.'' He pointed a pinky at his own chest.

Hercules looked up. He saw a wet blur; his eyes were heavy with tears. ''You knew?'' he asked. ''You knew I was lying?''

''Obviously,'' the general said. ''Too bad, though; I was really hoping that you two would take the poison to the Mercantilians.'' He shook his head sadly. ''Ah, well.'' The general began striding forward. The tent moved with him and swept past Hercules, moving toward the top of the ridge.

Hercules could feel Cactus growing cold in his arms. He pulled his hands away; his fingers were red and slick with the giant's blood. Cactus' mouth hung open, as if he were still surprised at Hercules; his were stained red. His eyes stared up, blank and blind.

Hercules watched the golden tent of ''Slaughterius'' waft past, heading up the ridge. He could imagine the general's face: callous and smug, like a schoolyard bully who had just beaten the smallest kid in his class and enjoyed it.

Vicius, with four of his soldiers, left the tent and surrounded Hercules. ''Get up,'' the captain commanded. ''The general can still use you, strong boy.''

Hercules shot to his feet. With a tiger's roar, he shoved past Vicius and sprang toward the general's tent. He ran inside, hungry to attack.

Within the tent, Vicius' other guards ran to defend their general, forming a double wall between him and Hercules. Enraged, Hercules grabbed them by the collars and necks, hurling them out of his way and into each other as he made his way toward his enemy.

Vicius whistled and kept walking. Twenty soldiers leaped from the ranks and hurtled into the tent. They piled onto Hercules; he slung them off, one by one, not caring where they landed or who got hurt.

He trudged toward ''Slaughterius,'' dragging one soldier who had wrapped arms around his knee, ignoring another who was pounding his back, and slamming a fist toward another who was hanging onto his shoulder but eluding his blows.

A few more steps, and the thin, white neck of "Slaughterius" would be in his hands. Hercules reached out to grab him. The soldier around his leg pulled it backwards; Hercules kicked him in the gut.

Slaughterius turned, glanced at Hercules, and looked at one of his tent holders. "Now," he said.

As one, the tent holders gathered up the fabric that shielded those beneath the canopy from the surrounding army. Hercules looked around. He could see that dawn was sliding over the sky toward him.

The Pastoralian army surrounded him. The semicircle was complete, curving from the ridge top to about a quarter of the way down the hillside, and every soldier in it was watching him.

The sun's rays touched his skin. For the first time, the Pastoralian army could see Hercules' face.

"Look at him, my soldiers!" the general shouted. "Look how he has his arms out to strangle me. Look how he has just kicked one of your brother Pastoralians in the belly. Look at the pile of soldiers he has already knocked cold—or dead!

"This is the man, the 'Hercules' "—he spat the name—"who came to our city to help us fight the Mercantilians—then took advantage of our hospitality, our food, our women!

"What shall we do to him?"

The thousand men rumbled, "Kill him!"

Hercules opened his mouth to speak, but the soldier on his shoulders clutched his hair and yanked, pulling his head backward. He grabbed the man's hands and tried to peel them off.

"Slaughterius" cupped a hand against his ear. "What was that?" he asked playfully.

"Kill him!"

He shook his head. "I'm so sorry. Can you repeat that just one more time?"

"**KILL HIM!**" It was a thousand-man roar.

"Slaughterius" stretched out his arms as if to sweep the entire army into one ecstatic hug. "Then do it, my brothers," he demanded. "Now—*do it!*"

A thousand howling soldiers broke ranks and shot toward Hercules. Their faces twisted with fury as they raised arrows, clubs, spears, whips, and torches. The pounding of their boots on the hillside thundered like a thousand cannons.

I'm in trouble, Hercules thought.

He spun like a top, hurling off the soldier around his shoulders. *I can't fight a thousand men at once. And the way they're going, they'll trample each other. I've got to get out of sight and let them calm down.* He ran toward the top of the ridge.

He bolted over the top, dropping beneath it and out of the soldiers' view. He ducked behind the biggest tree he could find.

The tree was as tall as the ridge itself, but its most startling aspect was its width. The tree was wider than the span of Hercules' outstretched arms; so broad was its trunk that it appeared on first glance as flat as a wall, and only a second look revealed that it actually curved like any other tree.

174

Temporarily safe, Hercules looked around to find more permanent lodgings. Instead, he saw an army.

Mercantilians, he thought. They stood only a few yards down the ridge, arranged in a giant square with more than thirty men on each side.

One man stood at the front and center of the square, like a fist atop a brick wall. Tall and muscular, he wore a gleaming silver breastplate and a tall helmet, with black plumes rising from its top.

Hercules recognized him immediately. *Ferocius,* he thought. *Uh-oh. He sees me.*

Ferocius turned to his army. "Men!" he shouted, "look at that man up there, the one in front of that big tree.

"That is the man we saw two nights ago. That is the man we befriended a week ago. That is the man who lied about being Hercules. That is the man who demanded our food and ale and women and obedience. That is the man who promised to come back with General Slaughterius' head."

He paused to let them hear the oncoming yells of the Pastoralian troops. "And now he's leading their army!" Hercules heard a rumble rise from the Mercantilian men, a growl of bubbling fury.

Ferocius thrust out an arm and pointed at Hercules. "Kill the traitor!"

The thousand-plus Mercantilians swept past their commander, rocketing up the hill with spears and swords in their fists. From the other side, the Pastoralian shouts grew louder.

Hercules turned; he looked around the tree. He saw the Pastoralian army hurtling toward him, only a few

175

seconds away from burying him under their thousand bodies.

How do I get into these things? he wondered as two thousand screaming men raced toward him from two directions. *And what's more, how do I get out?*

15

I've got no tools, no weapons, no—

He turned and looked at the enormous tree. He bent down and grabbed its thick, gnarled roots.

Hercules yanked. Leaning backward, bending his knees, arching his back, he began a slow, hard pull.

The tree slowly rose. Cascades of mud and dirt fell from its underside.

A squirrel scampered down the trunk and onto Hercules' head. It looked around, its claws digging into Hercules' scalp. He grimaced and tried to ignore the creature. The squirrel ran down his arm, leaped off of the back of his hand, and fled into the forest.

Hercules stumbled backward under the tree's weight. Leaves fluttered to the ground, and a thin branch broke off and fell, landing at the demigod's feet. Birds hurriedly flew out of the upper branches as a nest fell.

As he put one foot behind the other to gain his footing, Hercules could hear the soldiers on both sides backpedaling, trying to avoid having the tree fall on them.

On both sides, the soldiers regrouped and prepared to charge.

Hercules stepped to the top of the rise, carrying the massive oak. Straddling the ridge, with one foot on the Mercantilian side and one on the Pastoralian, he steadied himself and took a deep breath.

Here goes, he thought.

He whirled, wielding the tree like a club, sweeping Mercantilians and Pastoralians away like tenpins. As he paused, he could hear a mass of soldiers charging him from behind; again he spun, and again he knocked men back. They went rolling down the hillside, squealing.

The tree's weight and bulk made Hercules' arms ache. *I can't keep this going forever,* he thought. *But if I set the tree down, they'll overrun me.*

Two more gangs of troops attacked him, one from the right, the other from the left; he slammed the men on the left away, but the ones on the right barreled into him and nearly knocked him down. He had to swing the trunk of the tree onto their heads to stop them.

A hundred soldiers leaped at Hercules from all sides at once. He swung the giant tree, lashing most of them away, but a few Pastoralians got close enough to rip his legs with their clubs, and a few Mercantilians raked his back with their spears. The pain was blinding; he nearly passed out.

They're getting smarter, he thought as he slammed the tree into twenty more men. *And there are so many of them; I knock a dozen away, and there's still more than nineteen hundred running to kill me.*

From the corner of his eye, he could see crowds of Pastoralians huddled together, no doubt planning their next assault; bands of Mercantilians did the same. *I've got to do something now!*

He swung and spun, scanning the area for ideas. He caught an odd sight about a third of the way down on the Pastoralian side of the ridge, behind the soldiers: a straight row of a dozen trees, growing so close to one another that their trunks touched.

The sight troubled him. Trees in this forest, like trees in other forests, grew several feet apart, and almost never in a line. Moreover, he should have seen the trees before; he couldn't have missed seeing something so big and unusual as a wall of trees. Yet when he had gone from Pastoralis to the top of the ridge, and then looked down from the top, he never saw it.

He whipped his huge tree around again and stole a glance at the odd formation. There wasn't just one line of trees, he now saw; there were at least three. No, four, forming the walls of a close-packed square.

What he didn't see, he realized, were the soldiers' generals. Where was Ferocius? Where was "Slaughterius"? Why weren't they leading their troops?

Hercules spun, whipping his tree around in a wide circle, clearing away soldiers in every direction. Those he didn't knock down, backed away. He whipped the tree around faster and faster until the momentum nearly pulled it from his hands.

And then he let go.

The tree sped from his arms as if flung from the world's largest slingshot. It cannonballed through the treetops, shaking their upper branches and ripping leaves loose. It arced downward, hurtling like a falcon diving to grab a rabbit.

The soldiers of both armies watched it go. They couldn't help themselves; for a moment, they forgot about killing Hercules.

The tree plummeted, whistling through the air. Like a battering ram, it slammed through the front wall of the tightly packed square of trees, knocking it to the ground, shaking the entire forest; several Mercantilians and Pastoralians stumbled and fell. It was as if a giant's fist had hammered the ground.

Hercules and the armies saw the tree sticking out of the now-flat wall at a sharp angle. Bits of dirt flaked off and floated downward, highlighted in the yellow glow of dawn.

It worked! Hercules exulted.

Within the enclosure of trees, beyond the now-flattened wall, Ferocius and ''Slaughterius'' sat frozen in shock. Clouds of dust kicked up by the wall's fall settled over them. The top of the wall had landed inches from their feet. Had they been sitting closer, it would have crushed them.

Ferocius was sitting on the Pastoralian general's comfortable saddle, while ''Slaughterius'' sat on the back of his servant, who had arranged himself like an ottoman on hands and knees. Between them were the tray of delicate chocolates, a pair of wine bottles, and several parchment scrolls.

From behind the Mercantilian soldiers came a group of perfectly synchronized marchers. Hercules watched soldiers parting to allow an officer in a plumed helmet to march toward him, attended by a group of young guards.

The soldier was slim and his face unlined, but Hercules noted the dark circles of exhaustion under his eyes, the hard set of his mouth, and the white gash of scar tissue that lay on his otherwise sun-reddened right cheek. The man's iron breastplate was scarred and pitted in several places where knives, rocks, and other weapons had apparently tried to pierce it. His right hand held a firm grip on a lance; his left held a dagger. The smallest finger of that hand was an uneven stump. The man limped slightly as he approached.

"Honorius," Hercules said as the man and his entourage approached. Honorius nodded; he marched past Hercules and down the Pastoralian side of the ridge.

The Pastoralians, uncertain of how to react to the sight of their leader's dining with the enemy, parted as the Mercantilians had, and let Honorius approach the two generals. Hercules noticed that Honorius' son Peuris was part of his father's personal guard.

Ferocius rose and held out a hand to stop him. Honorius bent low. *Is he bowing?* Hercules wondered.

Honorious picked up the parchments that lay on the ground between the two men. He blew off some dust that had settled on them when the walls fell.

Honorius looked around, scanning the Pastoralian

troops. Vicius stepped forward, accompanied by a dozen subordinate soldiers. Honorius handed him the papers to read.

The two armies waited, so silent that Hercules could hear the pages rattle as Honorius and Vicius passed them back and forth. Hercules approached the foursome within the three standing walls.

He passed through the Pastoralian soldiers as if they were trees. No one disturbed him. Whether they were wary of his power, confused by the strange turn of events, or waiting for orders, he didn't know.

"Hercules!" Ferocius cried. The general leaped up, knocking the saddle sideways, and sprinted past Honorius and Vicius. He grabbed Hercules by the shirt front and pulled him forward. Hercules, amazed, stared into the man's fearful eyes.

"You'll understand," Ferocius said, his voice trembling. "You have to. Let me explain. It was him." He wheeled and pointed at "Slaughterius."

"He came to me," Ferocius went on. "You have to realize, ever since I was a kid, I wanted action, battles, masses of troops to deploy, like the great generals of history. But in Mercantilius, we didn't have an army. All we had was a police force. I had to settle for being chief of police. I felt so powerless." He paused, thinking. "No. Useless," he corrected.

Ferocius pointed at "Slaughterius" again. "Then *he* came! He didn't look like this, though.

"He said he'd give me a war. My people would need an army, and I'd be in charge. He said it'd be a huge military emergency, and in times of military emergency, generals get a lot of power.

"I could run Mercantilius. And I could lead battles like the great generals of history. I wouldn't even have to worry about getting hurt. He'd build walls around me if he had to. He said so."

Loudly, Ferocius added, "He said I had to do it. He forced me!"

He swung an arm wildly at the hundreds of tired and hurt young men. "And it came true. Look around.

"And there'd be more, he said. After this fight's over, he said, there'd be counterattacks that I could ward off and new battles that I could plan to pay the other side back for the counterattacks."

Ferocius' tone shifted from babbling to dreamy. "And he'd be gone," he continued. "Once this battle ended, he'd go back home. . . ." In a burst, he finished, eyes shining, "And I could conquer the whole island if I wanted!"

Ferocius gazed searchingly at Hercules' face. "You have to believe me," he said, "he forced me into the whole thing."

"No, he didn't," Honorius said. Vicius handed him a paper. "Your agreements with him are right here, plus notes and plans on how you made the agreements. Everything you said is true—except that 'Slaughterius' didn't force you into anything. From these papers, it looks like you were pretty eager."

Hercules heard a dark murmur, like the rumble of clouds before a downpour. The men on both sides were grumbling, their faces angry at the discovery that their leaders had betrayed them.

The soldiers began to step forward, slowly advancing on the generals. Hercules stepped between the men and their leaders. *I might have to save the generals' lives,* he thought, *and I'm not sure I want to.*

He stopped moving, startled at his own thoughts. *Generals?* he wondered. He stared at "Slaughterius," who glared back with hot fury.

"Slaughterius" isn't a general; he's an impostor. Ferocius said he didn't always look like this. What did he look like? Who would get anything good from all this murder and just leave it behind to let more killing happen? Who is he, really?

As soon as he asked himself the question, he had the answer. *Ares,* he thought. *Of course. "Slaughterius" is Ares. He loves this stuff. He set up this entire war.*

Hercules frowned as the men drew nearer. *Wait a minute. Ares can't transform his appearance. Maybe I'm wrong.*

But Hera could do it. Maybe he asked Hera to let him have the ability for a while.

The soldiers were only a few steps away now, rows of men in front of other rows in front of even more rows. There was no escape for Ferocius, Hercules knew. Nor for Ares.

Go ahead, Ares, Hercules thought. *Try something. You're good at making people warlike—but if you make these people more warlike, they'll trample you. You won't die, but I'll bet you'll hurt. Your only chance is to make them more peaceful.*

And you can't do that! You've never learned how to stop wars, only how to start them.

"Slaughterius" stood up. He began to howl. It was

a low wail, deeper than a wolf baying and louder than a gale-force wind.

Hercules froze. The hairs on his arms stood up, and a sudden chill raised gooseflesh all over his body. He found himself glancing over his shoulder, alert for trouble, suddenly nervous.

He looked at the men around him; they were feeling it, too. He wanted to run, to get as far away as possible.

Vicius broke. He bolted from the three-walled enclosure and shot into the crowd of soldiers, screaming.

Honorius followed, hurtling down the hillside, as did his guards, as did Peuris, as did Vicius' guards, as did Ferocius, as did hundreds and hundreds of soldiers. They scattered in every direction, like ants when hot water was poured on their anthill, stumbling and falling but getting up again and racing as fast as their legs could pump. They climbed over each other, pushed each other back, screamed at each other to get out of the way or get a lance in the gut.

Hercules was doing it, too. He chased blindly through the woods, not knowing where he was going, not caring, his feet thumping into the ground, his legs pushing him onward. He bumped into a tree but bounced off and kept running. He was fleeing nothing at all and not knowing why.

What's the matter with me? he wondered. *Ares can't do this. I'm not making sense. I'm just panicking.*

Panicking. He remembered a drunken demigod at a party, bragging about how his song frightened the gods' parents into letting Zeus take over Olympus. His singing induced his signature type of fear in the older king of the gods and made him run so that Zeus could take over.

Hercules braked, jamming his heels into the ground and nearly falling over forward with the force and suddenness of his stop. He turned and, in the face of a hundred men scrambling in his direction, began to run back up the ridge, returning to the tree walls.

A soldier slammed into him, fell to the ground, jumped up, and ran past him. Hercules could still hear "Slaughterius" singing, and he was still afraid. *I'm not ready for this*, he *thought. I was ready for Ares. I've dealt with Ares before. But I'm not ready for this one.*

He forced himself to keep going, shoving past soldiers who shoved past him. He ground his teeth together to keep them from chattering. *There's nothing to be afraid of*, he told himself. His heart was hammering. *This fear isn't real.* He gulped; his throat was dry. *This fear is just a lie.* His hands were sweating.

The soldiers were thinning out now. He could see "Slaughterius" alone in the enclosure, standing and swaying and singing. *Calm down!* he told himself, and paced forward.

Hercules took in a breath and hoped that his voice wouldn't tremble. He forced himself to look "Slaughterius" in the eye. He kept walking, afraid that if he stood still, "Slaughterius" would notice his knees knocking.

"You can stop singing now," he told the general, forcing his voice low. "You can't panic someone

186

who knows what's going on. And for the first time since I landed on this island, I know what's going on."

All of the soldiers had fled into the forest; the two men were alone. Now only a yard away from the still-singing general, Hercules stopped walking. "Take off the Slaughterius disguise, Pan."

The general stopped singing.

16

"Don't deny it," Hercules said. "I know what you've done."

In the woods around Hercules and "Slaughterius," the soldiers suddenly found their panic gone. They stopped running.

"You must have made a deal with Hera: she'd give you the power to transform yourself, and you'd use it to kill me."

The last soldiers to flee, the ones closest to Hercules and "Slaughterius," heard Hercules' voice.

"You knew that killing me wouldn't be easy. I've escaped death traps before. So you planned a death trap so huge that I couldn't escape it."

More and more soldiers turned and listened, fascinated by Hercules' revelations.

"First, you came to Ferocius, and you made your

deal with him. Then you turned yourself into a bunch of people on this island, one by one. You started spreading rumors about the Mercantilians and the Pastoralians. You made them hate each other.''

Soldiers tapped their comrades on the shoulders and told them to listen to Hercules.

"Then you turned yourself into me. You found the Mercantilians and acted like such a pig that they wanted to kill you. That is, to kill me.''

The soldiers who had run farther into the forest, no longer panicked, noticed that the soldiers closer in were staring at the generals' tree-wall enclosure. They headed back the way they had come and began to pick up Hercules' voice.

"When you left Mercantilius to go to Pastoralis with the Pastoralian spies, I think you made a side trip, maybe while they were sleeping. You turned yourself into the boatman who told Salmoneus and me about this place and brought us here.''

The soldiers ringed the opening of the tree-lined square, with more of them returning from the outskirts, like iron filings crowding toward a magnet.

"Then you turned back into me. You went to Pastoralis and made a pig of yourself so that they'd hate you—hate me—and want to kill me. At night, you knocked out the real Slaughterius and dropped him in his own dungeon. You turned into him and took his place.''

All of the soldiers were gathered in a ring around the two demigods.

"You made a deal with the forest nymphs to watch for trouble. That's why they kidnapped Cactus—you didn't want another Hercules impostor running around, muddying your plans to make the two towns think I was the worst man they ever met.''

The soldiers in the back of the circle tried to push toward the front while some soldiers shushed the others so they could hear what Hercules was saying.

''Of course, you had more than one plan to kill me. That's why you got the Pastoralians to lure me to their dungeon and poured acid on me and had Captain Vicius' men attack me.''

The soldiers were silent. The only sound was the chirping of a few birds, waking up in the dawn.

''But when my friends and I escaped, you went back to your first plan: you put me between two sides of a massive war. You risked the lives of two thousand men, and more. And when they found out your plans and wanted to punish you, you sent them panicking away from you. You made them so desperate that they didn't care if they trampled their best friends.''

Hercules stepped toward ''Slaughterius.'' He could feel the rising anger of the hundreds of men around him. A Zeuslike storm of anger was billowing up inside him.

''It won't work anymore, Pan,'' he said grimly. ''These men know what's going on now. You can't fool them and you can't scare them. You've failed.''

In a voice dripping with contempt, Hercules spat: ''Get out of our sight.''

''Slaughterius'' said nothing. He only smiled, his teeth gleaming in the sunlight. Even his skin was shining.

No, Hercules realized, not shining. Glowing. Hercules squinted and raised a hand to block the blinding beams shooting forth from "Slaughterius."

The man's skin cracked. Fissures opened between his fingers, down his palm, and up his arms. His flesh began to peel off his body, swirling downward in curlicue strips. As it fell, the skin drooped and softened and melted, dripping into sticky, pink puddles on the forest dirt. It gave off the sour, bitter stench of rotting mutton. The glow within the skin grew and became a tall oval, like an egg big enough to hatch a man.

Hercules heard someone laughing. The laughter was coming from inside the glow before him.

And then, quick as a handclap, it was gone.

Before Hercules stood a stocky little man—but not quite a man. The creature's legs, though as long as a man's, were shaped like a goat's hind legs, covered with fur the deep brown of mahogany. They ended in dirty, cloven hooves nearly covered by the melted flesh pooling on the ground.

Thick, kinky hair blanketed the creature's muscular chest. His coarse skin was tanned as dark as dirt. His torso bent forward, giving him a skulking, stealthy appearance, as if he were planning to scuttle away. A goatskin bag hung from a rope hooked around his waist.

It was his head, however, that caught Hercules' attention. The creature's hair was a curly, black bush, his eyes dark and glittering, his nose as long and curved as a buzzard's beak. His ears tapered to points; just above them, horns poked out of his temples, curved around the front of his head, and poked forward.

The creature grinned merrily. Several of its teeth were missing. Its tongue was long, not pink and rounded like a man's but red as blood and as pointed as his ears.

Hercules could hear the soldiers behind him gasping awe-struck comments. They had never seen a disguised demigod reveal himself before.

Hercules was not impressed. "I've seen better transformations, Pan. Now, beat it."

Without a word, Pan reached a knobby hand into his goatskin bag. He pulled out a set of pipes, seven wooden reeds bound together by vines. Each reed was a little shorter than the one next to it.

Pan raised the pipes to his thick lips. He began playing a quickstep dance, low in pitch at first but swiftly rising higher.

Beneath Hercules' feet, the ground rumbled and vibrated. He could see the soldiers looking around, searching for a safe place as the entire ridge quivered.

Leaves fell from trees; birds flew away, screeching in terror; branches broke off nearby trees, hitting the ground and the soldiers. An egg fell from a nest high in a tree and splattered at Hercules' feet.

As if new mountains were forcing their way up from underground, the soil around Hercules' feet began poking upward. Rough-sided, anthill-like cones of dirt rose as the ground continued to shake.

Hercules leaned against a tree to keep from falling, but the tree itself was quaking. He saw Pan, unmoved, still playing the strange tune, smirking behind his pipes.

The rising pyramids of earth split open, dirt spilling away from their tops. Something inside them was shoving their sides apart. Hercules saw trees, wider than houses, thundering up through the ground, pushing back heavy wedges of earth. As the trees shoved up from underground, their top branches sprang out, slapping Hercules' chin and scraping his nose. The trees shot upward, their leaves brushing his eyes.

Hercules stumbled backward into another tree. It, too, was growing, its rough bark scraping his back on its way up and lodging chips and splinters in his skin.

Shadows stretched over him. Hercules bent back, looking up, and saw the new treetops far above him, blocking the morning sunlight. He looked around; the trees were in a tight, nearly solid ring about him.

The trees stopped growing. Dust settled lazily to the ground. Hercules could hear the soldiers talking among themselves, trying to comprehend what they had just seen.

Hercules comprehended it. *Why didn't I see this coming? I saw that tight square of trees around Ferocius and "Slaughterius." I didn't hear it grow over the noise of the battle, but I should have realized how it got there.*

Pan did it. He's a fertility god. He can make things reproduce and grow.

Hercules cocked a fist. *Well, if he thinks a few trees are going to stop me. . . .*

The ground shivered again, and a new set of rumbles began. Hercules hit the ground.

A second round of giant trees, just outside the first, roared up from below the surface. As the new ring of trees rose, they wedged up the outer roots of the first group.

Hercules heard something groan. The trees of the inner ring were leaning forward. He looked up and saw the treetops bending toward each other—and down toward him.

The trees on the outside—they're pushing the inside trees over, Hercules realized. *They'll fall. They'll squish me like a bug.*

The creak and groan of trees being uprooted and the deep thunder of the quaking ground fell silent. The ground was still again. Hercules looked up; the trees were still angled dangerously close to collapsing onto his head, but they were no longer moving.

"Hercules," came the rough voice of Pan from the outside, "let's you 'n' me chat."

"I don't have anything to say to you," Hercules growled.

Pan laughed. It was a harsh sound, like a saw ripping through wood. "Aw, just gimme a chance. Y'know, I always liked ya, big guy. A little stuck-up, maybe—always looking down on the rest of us god types for messing with mortals—but a nice guy. 'Course, I never thought you were all that bright. . . ." He paused. "But now, that's changed. Ya did some fancy figuring, doping out my plans like ya did."

Pan's tone dropped lower, more confidential, even secretive. His voice grew louder; apparently, he was leaning in close. "Since you're so smart, I wanna give ya a new deal. Get this. I don't really wanna kill you. Like I say, I got nothin' against you.

"The guy I really don't like is ol' Zeus.

"Now, I know he's yer dad, but don't get all excited. You know us gods, we go up against our daddies a lot. Heck, Zeus did something like that when he took over Olympus."

Pan's tone turned mean and sharp. "And cheated me outa my place! *I* won that battle. Made the old king panic and run. But does Zeus seat me at his right hand? Oh, no. *I* get ignored like I was the water he used yesterday to wash dishes. If ol' High and Mighty washed dishes, which he doesn't. I gotta wash my own dishes. . . ."

Pan calmed himself. "Anyway. So, when Hera talked to me about wiping you out, I said sure. Nothin' personal, but I knew it'd make Zeus mad, which was fine by me." His voice went smooth and sinuous. "But, Herc, I didn't realize how sharp you were."

Hercules followed Pan's voice as it circled the trees; apparently, the goat god was pacing around him. "See, here's the deal. I pretend to kill you. I go up to Hera, she's happy, everything's great. You lay low for a while.

"Then you and me, we kill Zeus. Beats the heck out of just making him mad, ya know? You'd be perfect for the job; no one'd expect an attack by a guy everybody thinks is dead. I get my revenge, and—get this!—you get the throne!

"That's right, bud. You run Olympus. You're the guy for the job: the deposer of Zeus and his rightful heir. Me, I don't want the job; I hate running things. I'd rather spend time chasing forest nymphs, but *you* get the whole deluxe platter. You can run things your way. Get rid of Hera and Ares, make the gods stop picking on people, anything you want.''

Pan stopped circling. ''So . . . whaddaya say?''

Hercules wanted to throw up. Pan's offer was a naked bribe and probably a lie.

Hercules could believe that Pan hated Zeus and wanted him dead. He didn't believe that the other gods would let him take the throne. He didn't like them, and they didn't like him. Not that he wanted their throne anyway.

Besides, the idea that Pan or anyone else would even think him capable of such raw, greedy brutality disgusted him.

Hercules turned slowly, examining the trees leaning over his head. If he turned the offer down, Pan would send the trees crashing onto him.

But he couldn't accept, even if Pan's offer was sincere. The thought of deceiving the gods, killing his own father and setting himself up as dictator to the gods was repulsive.

There was one solution, he realized.

I could always lie. Pretend to accept the offer, then turn on Pan as soon as he frees me. Knock him cold. It'd be easy.

And it'd be wrong. Lying had caused all of the trouble of the past days, from the rising war between the two cities to the death of Cactus.

Still, it was the only way out. Lie or die.

''Hercules,'' Pan teased. ''I'm waiting. Yes or no.

Give me your answer, or the trees fall.''

Hercules took a deep breath. He knew what he had to do, and he didn't like it.

''No,'' he said.

17

Pan was silent for a long moment. Then, finally: "What?"

"I said no," Hercules declared. He felt new strength rushing into his body. "No more lies. No more deceptions. That game is over."

"You're darn right it's over!" Pan screeched. "You're over! You're *dead!*" He blew wild, shrieking blasts on his pipe, and the outer ring of trees began to rise again, pushing up the roots of the inner trees.

Hercules looked up. He saw the trees tremble and their branches shake as the rising new ring of trees pushed the older trees' roots completely into the air.

The older trees collapsed, their tops plunging at Hercules like vultures descending to devour a dog, the trunks falling toward him like hammers aimed to pound him into the forest floor.

Hercules leaped. Arms outstretched, he sailed toward the trunk of one of the new, still-rising trees. He grunted as he hit the hard oak and its fresh bark scratched his chest, but he ignored the pain. He hugged the trunk like a bear and squeezed his fingers into the wood. As the tree continued to ascend, it took Hercules with it.

Craggy, wooden claws ripped down his back. The oak in his arms had pushed up the roots of one of the older trees. The older tree's roots, now wholly out of the ground, had Hercules' skin on them.

Behind Hercules, a ground-level thunderclap exploded, and the woods shook. No, Hercules realized as the tree in his arms shivered, not an explosion, not a thunderclap. An impact. The older ring of trees had crashed into the ground.

Still holding the rough trunk, Hercules looked over his shoulder. To his left and right and behind him stood the newer ring of trees, now ten feet high but no longer growing. He looked down and saw the first circle of trees lying flat on the ground, their tops pointing toward each other and overlapping, their trunks radiating out like sunbeams. Dust clouds that the impact hurled into the air slowly settled toward the ground, lightly sanding the fallen trunks.

It worked, he thought. *I'm all right.* A breeze grazed his back and brushed the wounds that the fallen tree's roots had carved. The breeze made a flap of loose, bloody skin flutter like a flag, and Hercules winced against the pain. *Well, not completely all right, but—*

Something wrapped around him. It was roughly square but with rounded corners and sides. Thick tentacles grew from its edges, encircling Hercules and the tree. Its surface was soft and yielding, but there was a solid core within.

The thing snapped the tree's trunk off below Hercules' feet. He felt the thing carry him and the trunk through the air and turn him around.

Hercules peered around the trunk and saw a giant. The thing enveloping Hercules was the giant's hand, and the thing's tentacles were its fingers.

The giant stood twenty-five feet high. Coarse, matted hair covered its nude, muscular form; its skin was as red as hot embers. Its eyes glowered a glossy black, with red pupils. It had a mouthful of uneven fangs. Its breath, Hercules noticed as he winced and bent his head away, smelled as rancid as dead hogs.

The creature squeezed. Hercules gritted his teeth against the pain of those coarse fingers pressing his chest toward his back. The thing was trying to kill him.

"Knock it off, Pan," Hercules grunted.

The giant grunted in response, sending a new blast of stench into Hercules' face. He ignored it. "I mean it, Pan. I know this is you. It's just one of your disguises. Come on, giants don't just come out of nowhere. And you didn't expect me to forget you can change shape, did you?"

The giant paid no attention but kept squeezing. Perhaps it didn't understand speech. *Maybe I'm wrong,*

Hercules thought. *If Pan could turn himself into a giant to kill me, he didn't need to pull all those schemes. And why didn't he turn big before?*

Hercules looked down through a red haze of pain, hoping to spot a way out. He saw the two armies milling about, confused. The creature pounded down the steep hillside, its weight and bulk sometimes causing it to stumble and making soldiers scatter before it. *They look so scared,* he thought. *They—*

That's it!

He went on, "I can prove it's you, Pan. You're still trying to cause panic. Besides, no real giant slips when he marches down a hill. I know real giants; I've served in armies with them; some of them are my friends. And you're no real giant."

The giant kept its grip strong, but Hercules smiled. He was starting to roll with this subject. "Pan, why don't you stop putting on frauds? They never work. They—"

The giant roared in fury and squeezed tighter. Its palm tightened around Hercules' wounded back, scratching his flesh. *I think I got to him,* Hercules thought.

The giant's heavy fingers pinched Hercules' midsection; he could feel his ribs start to interlace and scratch each other. The giant's thumb and little finger were pushing Hercules' arms into the tree trunk. His skin was indenting the wood, cracking the bark inward. Hercules tried to push back, but with his palms pressed to the tree, he had no leverage.

If I don't get out of here quick, I'm going to die.

But I can't push him away. The only thing I can push is this tree.

Now, there's an idea. . . .

As the giant's fingers pressed in on him, Hercules pressed the tree. He gave the tree a hard squeeze, then a harder one.

It shattered.

Where there was once a tree, there was now only air filled with sawdust and splinters. The giant quickly tightened its grip, but grabbed nothing. Hercules had dropped away, neatly slipping through the space a tree had once filled.

Knees bent and hands outstretched to cushion his landing, he hit the forest floor softly and bounced upright. He turned and saw the giant's feet a few steps behind him.

Hercules grinned, faced forward, and ran down the hill. *Come and get me, you big phony!* The giant gave chase, its monstrous feet punching deep prints into the dirt. The ground bounced with its every pounding step.

Hercules glanced into the forest ahead. Before him stood a young maple, its bark smooth, its trunk strong and round and as wide as Hercules' palm. He sprinted toward it like a gazelle, with the giant closing in fast. He could see the giant's shadow covering him.

Hercules reached the tree, grabbed the trunk, and swung himself around it. He let go, the momentum of his swing slingshotting him at double speed back toward the sprinting colossus. He raced between the giant's feet, leaped up a full-grown oak, and launched himself like a cannonball at the back of one of the giant's massive legs.

He smacked the joint behind the giant's right knee, shoving the knee forward and making the running monster stumble. Hercules dropped to the ground, dashed in front of the giant, and shot toward the crucial angle where the foot joined the leg.

He hit hard, punching the foot backward just as the giant was trying to regain its footing. Collapsing in on itself, the creature fell face first and tumbled down the hill.

Future generations would marvel at the wide dent the creature made when it hit the heavy stone wall of Pastoralis. They could only guess, though, at the pain the impact caused. The giant screamed, and birds all over Peloponnesus fluttered in panic from their nests.

Now I know why he didn't turn himself into a giant before, Hercules thought. *He's a great schemer but a lousy colossus.* Hercules ran after the giant with both the Mercantilian and Pastoralian armies behind him.

He leaped from the ground to the creature's hand, ran up the arm, and stood on its face. He grabbed the woozy creature's eyelids and held them.

The rough beast raised a hand to slap Hercules away. "Don't do it, Pan," Hercules said evenly. "You've got two armies who'll be very happy to kill you if you try anything." The giant lowered its hand.

Hercules went on. "No more tricks, no more deceptions. If you tell me, 'Hey, behind you, it's a gorgon!' when there's no gorgon there, just so you can

swat me off your face when I'm distracted, I could—
well, I don't want to hurt you, but you know I'm
strong; if I don't have time to loosen my grip when
you send me flying . . ." He squeezed the eyelids a
little tighter.

The creature swallowed hard and tried to blink, but
Hercules held the skin flaps tight. "You . . ." the giant groaned. "You're . . . lying."

"He isn't, you know." The voice, calm and low,
came from up on the ridge. It was a richly feminine
voice, sweet and satiny. All of the men turned.

Dryope gracefully descended from the ridge top,
passing through the crowd of men without stopping,
as if she knew that they would part before she reached
them. Behind her trailed a line of her most beautiful
nymphs.

Dryope reached the giant's face and stroked its
sweating forehead. "Oh, Pan, Pan, Pan," she purred.
"Don't you know how honest Hercules is?" She
looked up at Hercules, smiled, and returned her gaze
to the giant. "If he says you'll be hurt, you'll be hurt.
Not everyone's a liar like you, dear heart." She
stopped stroking the giant; one of her nymphs rushed
forward, holding the hem of her skirt, and wiped the
giant's sweat from her queen's hand.

Dryope rose regally to her full height and shook
her head sadly. "You really do have to stop lying,
you know. I didn't mind so much when you came to
me as 'Slaughterius'—oh, don't look so surprised; of
course, I knew it was you. You were a fun little di-
version, actually. But now, because of you and your

lies, my forest has been shaking, and I really can't have that.''

She bent down and laid a kiss on his cheekbone. ''Farewell, Pan.''

With a thunderclap, a blinding column of white light burst down from the sky and covered the giant. The column receded into the blue as fast as it had come.

The giant was gone.

With a body no longer beneath him, Hercules tumbled to the ground. He pulled himself to his feet and stalked toward Dryope. ''You had no right to do that,'' he snapped. ''Pan hurt these people, and they have a right to try him.''

Dryope smiled at his anger and brushed his chest lightly with her fingertips. ''Oh, don't worry, cute man. I just sent him back to Olympus.

''Now, you know Hera; she'll be very angry at him for failing to kill you. She'll hunt him down, and she'll certainly punish him very badly. She'll do worse things to him than these poor mortals could do. You know that.''

The problem is, Hercules thought, *she's right. But that still doesn't give her the right to—*

''Hey!'' called a Mercantilian soldier. ''What about us?''

''He's right,'' shouted a Pastoralian. ''Our trade's still a mess, we don't have anyone running our towns—''

''I wanna go home!'' a Mercantilian cadet whined.

''So do we!'' a scratchy basso boomed. More soldiers from both sides joined in, turning the quiet morning air into a storm of demands and howls.

"Atten-*SHUN!*" shouted a rough voice, clear and loud over the crowd. The soldiers froze; most of them stood straight.

Vicius marched forward from the crowd. "At ease," he ordered, and the soldiers relaxed. He nodded at Hercules. "Go ahead."

"Me?" he asked. "I . . . uh . . ." He scanned the crowd, looking for a particular face, and found it in the front row of soldiers. "Honorius!"

The captain stepped from the Mercantilian side of the mob, curious. "Yes?"

"I need your advice," Hercules said. "How do you think we should handle things?"

Honorius fell silent and stared at the ground. Slowly, he began, "We have several problems, and shouting won't fix them. We need to put some leaders in place to handle them. In Mercantilius, we need a new mayor." He began to speak more firmly, picking up speed as he went. "Our old mayor's dead—he died not long after Ferocius put him under arrest and took over the town—and we're sure not going to trust Ferocius again."

"Darn right!" yelled another soldier. He and three comrades bulled through the crowd and, each holding a limb, presented the sad but struggling Ferocius to Hercules and Honorius. "He's under arrest, starting now!"

Hercules smiled. "Since you need a mayor," he said, "I nominate—Honorius."

Hundreds of faces turned to Honorius; he blushed.

"Your father was a mayor," Hercules went on. "You know how things run. You're a good man—and I think your people trust you." A cheer arose from a thousand Mercantilian throats.

"Okay, guys, okay," Honorius said, holding his hands up to quiet them, "but only 'til we can hold an election. All right?" Another cheer, louder this time.

"But what about us?" yelled a Pastoralian. "Who'll run our town?"

"Hey, Cap'n Vicius," yelled a member of his guard, "what about you?"

Vicius shook his head. "Nah. I'm just a soldier, guys. I can't run a city. Trade stuff, taxes, treaties—it's way beyond me. Hey, Herc, what about you?" He offered a hand. "I'm sorry I tried to kill you. No hard feelings, okay?"

Hercules shook his hand. "Sure. But I'm not the mayor type. I'm a traveling man. You'll have to get someone else."

"Mind if I apply for the job?"

Hercules thought that people seemed to love popping out of this crowd. The Pastoralians were murmuring a word that he couldn't quite believe.

The word was a man's name. Hercules gently pulled aside several soldiers who were in the way of the mysterious voice.

"Slaughterius!" Hercules shouted as he saw his dungeon ally making his way slowly to the front of the crowd.

"And what am I, chopped potatoes?" asked Salmoneus, walking behind the Pastoralian.

Hercules gathered each man in an arm and hugged them both. "You're all right! I didn't know what happened to you."

"Relax, Herc," Salmoneus grunted as Hercules squeezed. The demigod put the men down. "Vicius' guards took us to the city and kept an eye on us," Salmoneus went on. "We saw the whole thing from the guard station. When Pan disappeared, I talked the guards into letting us come back here."

"We're fine," Slaughterius agreed. He turned to the crowd. "My friends," he called out, "as you know, Pan took my place. But I am alive and well. If you want me to become mayor again, I will."

His humble tone left him, replaced by all-out determination. "And *this* time, I won't pay attention to rumors and lies about our friends, the Mercantilians!"

Two thousand men cheered. Honorius and Slaughterius shook hands, and the cheer rose louder.

"Well, you did it, Herc," Salmoneus said softly. "You stopped the war. I guess you'll move on, now."

"I think so, Salmoneus," Hercules said. "But you sound like you're not going to."

"Me?" The peddler grinned. "Heck, no! I got a job to do. See, Slotty and I were talking about it. These two cities may like each other now, but the other towns on this island still think they're a bunch of cheats, not to mention towns on the mainland. They need their image changed, and I'm just the guy to do it. It's a new business I just thought up. I call it an advertising agency." Hercules shot him a skeptical look. "Don't worry," Salmoneus said, "I won't tell any lies. See, here's the way it's going to work . . ."

"Later, Salmoneus," Hercules said. He made his way through the happily dispersing crowd and walked to the top of the ridge.

Dryope was there, alone, brushing her golden hair. "Hello, Hercules," she sniffed, not looking at him.

"Hello, Dryope," Hercules said. "I thought I was the one who was mad at you. What's your problem now?"

She wheeled. Her face was flushed with anger. "As long as you refuse to be my lover, you magnificent slab of man flesh, I will always be mad at you." She turned away and resumed brushing her hair, as calm as if she had never flared up. "But I don't think I'll try to hurt you anymore—at least, not for a while. Go back to your friends."

Hercules smiled to himself and shook his head. *Same old Dryope. Just can't get used to a guy turning her down.*

He headed along the top of the ridge. The morning sun was bright, but the air was still comfortably cool. The birds, returning to the forest after the shocks of battles and instant trees, twittered sweetly.

Down below, he could see Salmoneus trying to talk Honorius into hiring him to improve Mercantilius' reputation. Slaughterius was deep in conversation with Vicius, apparently working out details for keeping order in Pastoralis. Soldiers were returning home or talking with each other; Hercules was pleased to see Pastoralians mingling with Mercantilians.

I'm glad everything turned out all right, he thought. *I just wish that you could be a part of it.*

You were always honest with me. You never told me even the smallest fib. You were a true friend—true in every way.

Goodbye, Cactus.

XenA

WARRIOR PRINCESS™

__**THE EMPTY THRONE** 1-57297-200-9/$5.99

A novel by Ru Emerson based on the Universal television series
created by John Schulian and Robert Tapert

__**THE HUNTRESS AND THE SPHINX**

1-57297-215-7/$5.99

A novel by Ru Emerson based on the Universal television series
created by John Schulian and Robert Tapert

__**THE THIEF OF HERMES** 1-57297-232-7/$5.99

A novel by Ru Emerson based on the Universal television series
created by John Schulian and Robert Tapert

Coming in May 1997: **PROPHECY OF DARKNESS**
1-57297-249-1/$5.99

VISIT THE PUTNAM BERKLEY BOOKSTORE CAFÉ ON THE INTERNET:
http://www.berkley.com/berkley

Payable in U.S. funds. No cash accepted. Postage & handling: $1.75 for one book, 75¢ for each
additional. Maximum postage $5.50. Prices, postage and handling charges may change without
notice. Visa, Amex, MasterCard call 1-800-788-6262, ext. 1, or fax 1-201-933-2316; refer to ad # 693

Or, check above books Bill my: ☐ Visa ☐ MasterCard ☐ Amex _____ (expires)
and send this order form to:
The Berkley Publishing Group Card#_____
P.O. Box 12289, Dept. B   Daytime Phone#_____ ($10 minimum)
Newark, NJ 07101-5289   Signature_____
Please allow 4-6 weeks for delivery. Or enclosed is my: ☐ check ☐ money order
Foreign and Canadian delivery 8-12 weeks.

Ship to:

Name_____	Book Total $_____
Address_____	Applicable Sales Tax $_____ (NY, NJ, PA, CA, GST Can.)
City_____	Postage & Handling $_____
State/ZIP_____	Total Amount Due $_____

Bill to: Name_____

Address_____ City_____

State/ZIP_____